SWING OF YOU...

Christopher looked at Robin and wished that he could take her in his arms and keep her there forever. She was adorable. She looked very young and slender in the pale, delicate dress, and her head in the lamplight had the sheen of a raven's wing.

His fingers closed over hers.

'Oh, my sweet,' he whispered, 'if only we were alone together – I'd like to kiss you until you were breathless.'

Robin did not answer but she looked at him. There were two little answering flames in her hazel eyes, and her heart raced and shook.

Swing of Youth

Denise Robins

CORONET BOOKS
Hodder Paperbacks Ltd., London

Copyright © 1930 by Denise Robins
First published in Great Britain
by Mills & Boon, Ltd., London
Coronet revised edition 1972

Printed and bound in Great Britain for
Hodder Paperbacks Ltd,
St. Paul's House, Warwick Lane,
London, E.C.4
by Hunt Barnard Printing Ltd,
Aylesbury, Bucks.

ISBN 0 340 15809 3

SWING OF YOUTH

CHAPTER I

ROBINA FRAYNE – known to all and sundry as Robin – sat on the window-seat in the sitting-room of a little, newly built house and flattened her nose against a window pane, rather like a small child.

She was small and thin and perhaps her very bright eyes, which were a beautiful warm hazel, and the swift movements of her charming dark head and pretty hands had rightly earned for her the contraction of her real name. She was eighteen and looked even younger.

Robin felt frankly fed up with everything today. To begin with it was a beastly day. It was pouring with rain. She was supposed to be looking at a garden. But there were only oblongs and circles of mud with one or two green blobs, meant to be plants. Frank, Robin's brother-in-law had planted them. Everybody hoped that flowers would appear in the fullness of time.

To Robin – whose one dream in life was a cottage in the country – real country like Sussex – the wretched little garden which Frank and Enid cherished wasn't a garden at all. She hated it. She hated 'The Rosary', this semi-detached house which Enid and Frank thought the last word in modern comfort. She thought it hideous. That was because there were hundreds of others exactly like it and with names like 'The Rosary' in this new estate in Shelbury, on the outskirts of London.

Enid was always telling Robin that she ought to be glad to have a roof over her head, and Frank – a pompous little man – put in his spoke when there was an argument and said,

'There are thousands worse off than you, my dear.'

Robin could not tolerate the idea of such a marriage as

Enid had contracted with Frank Latimer. She wanted a thrilling lover who would be a friend.

Of course it would have been so much better if Robin had been allowed to earn her own living. She did not want to be dependent on Frank and Enid. But, unfortunately, a year ago – two years after Enid's marriage and just as Robin had left school – Enid fell ill. An operation left her delicate. Both she and Frank considered it Robin's duty to come and help her in the house and look after her. They might have paid someone to come in and help. But they didn't think of that. That was a year ago. Enid was much better but Robin was still here and whenever she tried to get away, Enid begged her to stay and said that it would be ungrateful of her to go off now after all she and Frank had done for her.

On this cold February afternoon Robin flattened her small nose against the window pane and looked desolately at a desolate sky, and told herself that she was a little idiot. Too chicken-hearted. Of course she ought to get away from Enid and Frank and make her own life. But as soon as Enid started appealing to her or producing a sudden new pain, Robin stifled her own ambitions and promised to stay on.

It was getting darker every minute. The end of a dreary afternoon. Enid had gone to the West End to meet her husband 'for a cup of tea at Lyons and a bit of shopping'.

They were due back at half-past six. Supper was ready.

So Robin had nothing to do and she was bored, oh, how bored!

She felt that she could not sit here alone and brood a couple of hours until Frank and Enid came home. There wasn't even a dog here for a companion. She wanted badly to buy a Cairn terrier of her own. She loved Cairns. But Enid wouldn't have a dog in the place because 'they messed up the place and made work with their muddy paws' and disturbed the peace of her orderly, well-run home. So like Enid!

Robin felt that she must go out. She was in a rebellious mood today. So she put on a beret which fitted closely over her small, dark head; a green nylon mac, and her thickest shoes. Despising an umbrella she walked out into the rain.

She left the residential area behind her and came to Shelbury High Street. Crowded, dark, dismal in the February rain, more dismal than usual, since it was early closing day and most of the shops were shut.

'I ought,' thought Robin, 'to remember Frank's wonderful words that there are thousands worse off than I am, but I'm beginning to wonder what could be worse? I suppose I might be crippled, or always ill, or blind or something. But thinking that way doesn't seem to help much. I'm a coward, that's what I am. I want the excitement of being on a battlefield where one can be noticed and perhaps get a V.C. And really, it's much braver to drudge along in this sort of way and help Enid and save money for Frank, than to be a heroine in the public eye!'

With these noble thoughts, Robin – quite aware that she wouldn't feel noble for long – raised her face to the grey skies and stepped off the curb to cross the road. A foolish thing to do. A long, blue and silver car being driven, certainly, at unpardonable speed for Shelbury High Street, was upon her before she was aware of it. The very latest and most efficient four wheel brakes pulled the car up magnificently. Robin sprawled in the gutter, her purse flying into space. Ignominiously she lay there, more dazed and shaken than hurt, though her left arm hurt acutely.

The next thing was that she was being helped on to her feet by the man who had been driving the blue and silver car. A rather curt voice said,

'You should look where you're going!'

Robin put a hand to her cheek. It was smeared with mud, but not blood, she noticed thankfully. Half in tears she answered,

'I'm sorry – but you were driving awfully fast.'

'Are you hurt?' asked the man. He still held her right arm. She was trembling all over. A crowd – the usual inquisitive kind – gathered. It seemed to annoy him. 'You'd better jump in and let me drive you back,' he added.

'No, I'm all right,' said Robin faintly. 'You hit my arm – but I don't think it's broken.'

He looked down at her. They were standing underneath a

street lamp and he suddenly noticed that his victim was a young and extremely pretty girl. Aubrey Mauldron was a connoisseur of pretty women. He saw in the face of this one, two things rarer than beauty. Innocence and a hint of sensuality. She was trying to smile, which exhibited the two fascinating clefts in her cheeks.

When he spoke to her again, his voice had lost its brusqueness. His manner was at once tender and charming. Nobody could be more charming than Aubrey when he chose.

'You poor little thing, it was criminal of me to drive so fast. I insist upon taking you home. You're shaken up – and no wonder. Jump in and tell me where to go.'

Robin was dazed and embarrassed.

She made a feeble protest but nevertheless allowed herself to be helped into the car. She knew she was glad when she found herself in that warm, luxurious limousine. She leaned back and sighed, and closed her eyes.

'I feel a bit sick,' she said.

Aubrey Mauldron gave her a startled look.

'My dear little girl, you won't be sick in my brand new Alfa Romeo, will you?' he asked laughing.

She found herself echoing the laugh, feebly.

'No, I promise I won't, but I do feel awful.'

'The shock's upset you. Just sit still. Where do you live?'

'Shelbury, on the new estate,' said Robin. 'If you go straight on and take the first turning to the right it will get us there. The house is called "The Rosary". I'll show you. It's awfully kind of you . . . '

'Not in the least,' he said. 'Considering that I did my best to kill you.'

'You haven't succeeded in doing that.'

'Thank God,' said Aubrey warmly.

He turned the car off the High Street and down the road as she directed, and so they came to 'The Rosary'. Scarcely half an hour had elapsed since Robin left home, bored and wretched. Now she returned in a glorious car having narrowly escaped death. She still felt dazed.

The house was in darkness. Enid and Frank had not yet

returned. Robin hesitated to invite a complete stranger into her brother-in-law's house, yet she felt that it would be rude of her not to do so, since he had taken the trouble to drive her home.

'Won't you come in for a moment,' she said as he helped her out of the car.

'If you're sure I shan't be a bore, I'd like to come and satisfy myself that you're all right,' he said.

'I am – it's only my arm – but I'm sure it isn't broken,' she said.

She led the way up the garden path, past the flower beds which were now all pools and puddles and sodden, dejected plants. She opened the door with her latch key, switched on the lights in the hall and the sitting-room and then faced the man who had run her down.

She saw a very good-looking man who might be any age between thirty and forty. He had dark hair with just the touch of grey at the temples which a woman finds attractive; regular features and very blue eyes. Irish eyes, Robin decided at once, and later discovered that she was quite right. Aubrey's mother had been Irish.

He was well-groomed, just a little too debonair and smart, perhaps. But he was definitely handsome, a gentleman, and had delightful manners. Only those who knew Aubrey Mauldron well, and particularly the women who knew him too well, were aware that there was sheer cruelty behind the charming mask. The hot Irish blood which ran in Aubrey's veins could make of him a fiend at times. It was a fiend nearly always conjured up by women. He controlled himself amongst men.

He was his most delightful and sympathetic to Robin this afternoon.

'You look pale, poor poppet,' he said, putting his coat and hat on a chair. 'Do let me have a look at the arm.'

Robin allowed him to help her off with the mac. She rolled up the sleeve of her pullover. There was a big, ugly bruise near the shoulder, rapidly swelling and assuming a purple, mottled hue. The skin was bruised. Robin grimaced.

11

'Beastly, isn't it?' she said.

'It's horrible – I'm most fearfully sorry,' said Aubrey fervently. He held her hand and looked not at the bruise but at the ivory whiteness of the slender arm below that bruise.

'Can't we bathe the arm or something?' he asked.

'No, not now – my sister will be home in a moment – she'll see to it for me,' said Robin, feeling not quite truthful because Enid couldn't bear the sight of a bruise or a cut and said it made her turn faint.

'The only good point about this accident,' he said, smiling at her, 'is that it gives me the pleasure of meeting you, Miss – '

'Frayne,' she finished for him, 'Robin Frayne.'

'Robin?' he repeated, raising his brows.

'Well, it's really Robina, but the family have always called me Robin,' she explained.

'I think it's charming and so unusual,' he said.

He thought her charming. There was nothing blasé about her. She was a fresh, old-fashioned little thing. Yet she didn't seem suburban like this dreadful box of a house. He introduced himself.

'My name's Aubrey Mauldron – just back from Morocco – amazing place – wonderful trip – came home through Spain. Wonderful, full of colour and poetry.'

Robin pricked up her ears and forgot the pain in her arm. Morocco! Spain! Colour and poetry. Were these things not her secret dreams? She broke into excited questioning about Mr. Mauldron's recent travels. He answered each question and seemed amused to do so.

Aubrey was a good conversationalist. He was also very vain, and it flattered him to have such an enraptured audience.

'What an intense little thing she is,' he mused. He immediately pictured her being intense about him, rather than his travels. He was tired of the beautiful, model girl with whom he had been having an affair for the last six months.

Aubrey Mauldron was by no means a cold sensualist. Generally he imagined that he fell in love – hotly and very rapidly in love.

12

Half an hour in the sitting-room of 'The Rosary', talking to Robin Frayne, sufficed to make him believe that he was in love again. He intended to see more of this girl.

'And do you mean to tell me that you live here with your sister and brother-in-law and must do housework and that sort of thing,' he said in a shocked voice.

Robin explained that Enid was delicate and Frank hard up.

'Life can't mean anything to you,' he said. 'It must be too dreary for words.'

'Well, it is, I suppose, at times,' Robin admitted. 'Frankly I'd much rather be earning my own living somewhere.'

'No,' said Aubrey, 'You ought to have somebody looking after you and giving you a wonderful time.'

'Why should they?' laughed Robin.

'Because you're wasted here – you're like the incarnation of Spring – like a linnet or a swallow or a robin' – he laughed – 'a real robin in a cage.'

Her pulses thrilled curiously. She felt quite depressed when he stood up and said that he must go because he had a dinner engagement – early dinner because he was going to a show.

He mentioned the name of the play and asked her if she had seen it. She said no. He discovered that she hadn't seen any of the plays running in town at the moment. She never went out to a dance – or anything but an occasional cinema. Aubrey was charmed.

'Would you think it frightfully impertinent of me if I suggested that we should meet again,' he said as he took his leave. 'I mean – that horrible bruise on your arm – I feel so guilty – so remorseful. I'd like to prove it – perhaps you'd do me the great honour of coming out with me for a drive in the wretched car that knocked you down.'

He was smiling. The Irish blue eyes were very attractive and sincere at this moment. It is not to be wondered at that she said, weakly, 'Yes, of course, I'd like to see you again, sometime.'

And that for her was just the beginning of – she knew not what. But for Aubrey Mauldron it was more than the begin-

13

ning. It was half the battle won. He knew that he was clever enough to make a conquest of an inexperienced girl like Robin Frayne and to make it without difficulty. It wasn't fair play. She wouldn't have a chance and he knew it. But it didn't prevent him from going ahead. Whatever else he was, Aubrey Mauldron was not and never had been a sportsman.

CHAPTER II

EXACTLY one month later when the cold March winds were blustering across Shelbury and scattering the yellow petals of the crocuses which were Frank Latimer's pride, Robin and her sister had what might be termed a good row.

Enid wanted to go to a West End theatre with her husband. And on this particular night Aubrey Mauldron had taken tickets for a revival of *Bitter Sweet*.

Robin had looked forward to *Bitter Sweet* almost passionately. She loved music and by this time she had learned to love going out with Aubrey Mauldron.

A few days ago Enid had told her that she had better not see so much of Mr. Mauldron. It didn't seem right to her. Robin – having tasted the honey of an amusing and thrilling time with Aubrey – scoffed at this.

'I'm eighteen and I can take care of myself,' she declared.

The whole complexion of life had altered for Robin since Aubrey's advent. She had something to look forward to now; drives in his car; an occasional theatre; a good film. He had even taken her one afternoon to catch a glimpse of the Sussex Downs, beloved of her dreams.

She wasn't going to give up Aubrey's friendship just because Enid and Frank were narrow-minded and considered it improper.

The row this afternoon between the sisters evolved from Robin's announcement that Aubrey was taking her to *Bitter Sweet*.

'He's doing nothing of the kind,' said Mrs. Latimer tartly. 'Frank's taking me to a West End play and I'm not going to have the house left empty after that burglary down the road.'

'And I'm not going to be turned into a caretaker and miss

15

my bit of fun!' said Robin heatedly.

Enid blushed with anger at this. She lost her temper and told Robin that she was an ungrateful little beast.

'Ever since that wretched Aubrey Mauldron has been buttering you up with his attentions, you've been impossible, Robin!' she finished furiously. 'Neglecting Frank and me and the home. A home we've given you, mind you. If it wasn't for us you'd be living in some squalid bed-sitter and –'

'Please, Enid,' interrupted Robin, 'remember that I've always wanted to be independent and earn my own living and make my own life and you wouldn't let me go.'

'I suppose you'll be flinging it down my throat that I'm delicate and you've had to nurse me!' said Enid. 'Frank said last night –'

'I don't care what Frank said,' said Robin, her lips mutinous. 'I've a right to get what I want out of life as well as you. I do all the housework here. Isn't that enough? Honestly, Enid, I can't see why you should begrudge me a little pleasure.'

'I wouldn't mind if something decent was going to come out of this friendship between you and your expensive boy-friend,' said Enid. 'But Frank and I think he is just a playboy.'

'You've no right to say such a thing. He's always been most polite and nice and –'

'And where's it leading to?' broke in Enid. 'Do you imagine a man with his money will want to marry a girl like you?'

The blood flew to Robin's cheeks now.

'There's no question of that, Enid.'

'Don't deny that you're keen on him,' said Enid coarsely.

Something seemed to hurt deep down in Robin then.

'Don't let's discuss Aubrey, Enid,' she said quietly. 'It's about tonight. You want me to give up my show. It isn't fair. Aubrey has booked seats and I've been looking forward to it and you've only just sprung it on me that you are going out with Frank.'

'You're nothing but a selfish little wretch!' said Enid vindictively. 'I won't have "The Rosary" left at night. It's my

16

home and you're my young sister and if it's a question of who's to give up going out, it ought to be you.'

'It's always me,' protested Robin. 'And this time I'm not going to give in, Enid. I'm going to *Bitter Sweet* and nothing shall stop me.'

Enid's face went livid. She was a hot-tempered young woman and she lost her control in the face of her young sister's defiance.

'I'm not going to stand this sort of thing from you, Robin,' she said. 'I don't see why I should. If you go out with that man tonight, you can pack your things in the morning and make a home somewhere else. I've had about enough of you.'

'Enid!' exclaimed Robin. 'How can you be so unfair?'

Enid marched to the door.

'You heard what I said and Frank will endorse it, I know.'

'Very well,' said Robin, her heart beating quickly. 'I'll go. I've always wanted to make my own life and now I shall.'

Enid turned at the doorway, two spots of red on her sallow cheeks.

'And who's going to finance you, might I ask?' she said. 'Your boy friend, perhaps? Frank and I won't give you a penny.'

Robin's heart sank. It was all very well sighing for freedom and here was the chance she had wanted. It was a painful way of parting from her sister and brother-in-law, but it meant freedom if she cared to take it. On the other hand the dread question of money had to be considered. Enid had only given her enough to buy the bare necessities of life. She hadn't saved a penny.

However, she refused to be defeated by Enid. She was not going to miss *Bitter Sweet*. Besides, she looked forward so intensely to being with Aubrey.

She was certainly in the mood to be melted by *Bitter Sweet* – to be affected by any emotion when she finally joined him that evening.

He noticed at once that she was pale and subdued when he called for her in the Alfa – driven by his chauffeur tonight. She was, as a rule, enchantingly gay. He was crazily in love with her – as far as Aubrey Mauldron was capable of being in love. And that was not the best way because he had no intention of giving up anything for her. It was she who would have to give up everything for him.

He had been clever with her. He would like to have shown his hand at once but he knew that there was a romantic streak in Robin Frayne, she would want wooing. He had waited his chance. Tonight it had come.

'My dear,' he said, in that voice which he could make so rich with tenderness. 'Something's the matter – you aren't yourself. What's wrong?'

Robin bit her lip.

'I've had a row.'

'With your sister?'

'Yes. Enid's been unfair and horrid. She said if I came out with you tonight I could get out altogether.'

Mauldron fingered his white tie and his lips curved into a line of pleasure. What could be better than this? The gods were on his side.

'But this is iniquitous,' he said. 'What's occasioned such a thing?'

Then the story tumbled out. Robin was thoroughly upset – worried because she had openly defied her sister although she thought she was justified. She told Aubrey everything and finished up by saying,

'You see – Enid and Frank don't think that I – that you –'

She broke off, scarlet, long lashes hiding the embarrassment in her eyes. She was so essentially clean and decent, she felt that it was an insult to Aubrey Mauldron to suggest that their friendship bore criticism.

Aubrey looked down at her through half-shut eyes.

'This is unbearable, Robin,' he said. He took her hand and held it tightly between his own. Her cold, nervous little fingers instinctively clung to his. 'You can't go on with that ghastly life under your sister's roof. You weren't meant for it.'

Robin's heart began to beat so fast that it frightened her. She was frightened of the emotion roused in her by the fierce clasp of his hands. She tried to laugh.

'Goodness knows what I was made for!'

That gave him a wonderful opening.

'Do you know that old song little Robin? . . . "You were meant for me and I was meant for you – Nature patterned you and when she was done, you were all the sweet things rolled into one! . . ." '

The blood was drumming in her temples now.

Speechlessly she looked up at the man. His Irish blue eyes were amazingly kind – encouraging. He was much too adept to rush like a bull in a china shop.

'You were meant for me,' he repeated. 'Robin, my dear, you aren't going to have to worry any more – you aren't going back to that deadly life at Shelbury. Tomorrow morning you must pack a suitcase and come with me. Do you hear, sweetheart, you must come with me – where you belong!'

Just for a moment she hung back – trembling on the precipice, enthralled yet afraid.

'Oh, how can I – what do you mean –'

'Don't you understand,' he said. 'I love you. I'm madly in love with you, you little birdlike thing. Don't you care for me, Robin? Is it that you don't like me?'

She answered that at once with her innate sincerity.

'Yes, I do love you, I do. I can't deny that.'

'Robin!' He caught her in his arms now, regardless of the traffic and the lights in the busy thoroughfare around their car. 'You darling! You little darling baby thing!'

She felt his lips upon her mouth. It was a long kiss which seemed to drain away her very heart's blood.

'Listen, Robin,' he said, when he drew his lips away from hers. 'How much do you love me? How much do you trust me?'

'Absolutely,' she said.

'Enough to come to Paris with me tomorrow?'

'To Paris?' Her large hazel eyes looked up at his, startled.

'Yes, it's like this. I've got to go to Paris tomorrow. I've got a business engagement. I can't put it off. Have you got a passport?'

'Yes. I went abroad with a party from school three years ago.'

'Then come with me and we'll get married over there.'

'Married,' repeated Robin and laughed shakily.

'Of course,' said the man carelessly and touched her warm cheek with his forefinger. 'Oh, my little darling, your dimples send me quite crazy. Smile at me. Let me kiss them.'

She was in his arms again, blind, deaf to everything on earth but his love and this lover.

'You've been a slave in your sister's house quite long enough,' said the insidious voice of Aubrey in her ear. 'Serve them right, my dear, if you do quit and quit without telling them where you are going and what you are doing. All I want you to do is to meet me in the morning. We'll drive to Heathrow and fly to Paris. How does that appeal to you?'

She drew away from his arms.

'Aubrey – you're asking rather a lot – it's a big thing for me to break away from my family and go abroad with you. I'm not a conventional prude or anything like that but – '

'I know exactly what you feel about it, darling,' he broke in. 'But one can be married in Paris as easily as in London. More easily. I've got a flat over there – a place you'll love. And if you'll trust yourself to me, you'll be all right, Robin, and we'll get married the next morning.'

'I ought to say no,' she whispered, 'but I do trust you absolutely, Aubrey, you've been so good to me ever since that night your car knocked me down.'

He might have felt ashamed of himself in that moment. But he was past shame.

'I'll take care of you, Robin, my sweet,' he said, and kissed her dimples again and then her lips, until she was weak and powerless to protest. She took it for granted that he would marry her.

Then Aubrey played his trump card.

'Of course, my dear baby, if you don't believe in me or if you think your family right in diagnosing me as a villain, you have only to tell me so and we'll say goodbye at the end of this evening. I'll go to Paris and try and forget you.'

That terrified her.

'No, no, don't do that – don't go away without me, Aubrey.'

'Then you will come with me tomorrow?'

They had reached the theatre. She saw the words *Bitter Sweet* flashing in electric lights. She clung closer to the man she loved, feeling that life to her was incredibly sweet and that there must never be any bitterness.

'In this play a girl elopes with her lover, Robin,' Aubrey said as he helped Robin out of the car, 'but it ends in tragedy. Our story mustn't do that, must it, darling?'

She looked up at him, her heart racing so fast that it hurt her.

'It never will,' she said.

She walked into the theatre with him like one who sees heaven before her. And as yet she had no knowledge that there is a special little hell as well as a heaven reserved for women who love.

CHAPTER III

A VERY long time was to elapse before Robin Frayne saw her
sister Enid again. Enid and Frank were already home, in bed
and asleep by the time Aubrey brought Robin back. And that
next morning, very early, before the Latimers were awake,
Robin said goodbye to 'The Rosary'.

Aubrey had said that when they were married he would buy
her all the clothes she needed. So she took only a small suitcase with her.

She had left a letter for Enid telling her that she had run
away and that was all. She could picture Frank's righteous
indignation and Enid's scathing remarks. But neither of them
would really regret her except that they had lost a good cook!

The rest of the day seemed to Robin like a dream from
which she would soon awake. Aubrey did everything well.
They flew to Paris first class. Robin found that air travel
made her feel sick. She was silent and miserable until they
reached Orly.

She was very ashamed of her malaise but Aubrey laughed
and teased her. She thought there couldn't be any man in the
world half as nice as Aubrey. Yet by the time she was in Paris
she was rather silent and preoccupied. She had burned her
boats so completely by going abroad like this, and perhaps
she had not realised until now how infinitely she had trusted
Aubrey by coming with him in this way.

She stood beside him in the Customs shivering a little
whilst he talked to a gesticulating porter in perfect French.
Then she found herself in a taxi tearing through the streets
of Paris.

Aubrey looked down at her. He felt irritated because she
was so subdued. He could not tolerate depression and he

liked Robin in her gay, birdlike moods.

'Cheer up, sweet,' he said. 'Why so silent? We're in Paris. We've left London and Shelbury behind us. And you're going to have the most marvellous time in your life.'

His rich voice had the immediate effect of cutting those two delicious clefts in her cheeks.

'I think I'm a bit tired, Aubrey – and just a bit over-whelmed by what I've done.'

'You've been splendid,' he said tolerantly. 'Don't start regretting it now.'

'I don't – of course I don't. But –'

'You're not going to disappoint me by saying you won't be happy till we're safely married, are you?' He could not resist sneering a little.

At once she was flung into a panic because she thought she had offended him.

'Aubrey! Don't!' she protested. 'I can't bear you to talk to me like that. It's never entered my head you won't marry me.'

He put an arm round her. He was bored with this but he raised each of her hands in turn to his lips.

'Enchanting, and what would you say if I told you I wasn't really a marrying man?'

She felt her heart miss a beat but managed a laugh.

'You're kidding me,' she said.

He frowned. Somehow, Robin, more than any girl he had known, had the power of making him feel uneasy. But he laughed and whispered,

'I'm crazy about you,' and kissed her until she was breath-less.

'I adore you, Aubrey,' she said and the tears sprang to her eyes.

'Glad you're in Paris with me?' he asked.

'Yes, terribly glad.'

'I'll be good to you,' he said quickly. He meant it. But his ideas of goodness were not hers.

Holding her tightly in his arms, he pointed out the beauties of Paris as they flashed past in the March dusk. When they came to the Madeleine – Aubrey said in a casual voice,

'Look here, sweet, do you mind calling yourself Mrs. Mauldron when we get to the flat? My valet, Henri, might think things if you stay there as Miss Frayne. Tomorrow you'll be Mrs. Mauldron really!' He smiled at her. 'I know you trust me and I don't want Henri gossiping.'

Robin nodded, her cheeks hot. There were tired shadows under her eyes.

'I understand.'

'And I'm going to put this ring on your finger,' he added, and hastily drew a small platinum ring from his pocket.

Robin felt hot when he slipped the circlet over her finger.

'I don't quite like it,' she laughed. 'I'm a bit superstitious about wearing my wedding ring before my wedding.'

'I can't allow that, sweet,' said Aubrey gaily. 'Superstition is the cult of the ignorant. You've got brains, my child.'

Robin unfortunately did not use those brains that night. He kissed the ring when it was on her finger and joked with her.

'There you are, Mrs. Mauldron!'

'Oh, Aubrey, don't!' she said, half thrilled and half afraid.

The next excitement was Aubrey's flat. A wonderful penthouse with windows which seemed to look over the whole of Paris. They were quite close to the river. It moved slowly and darkly under the old bridges. Robin was thrilled by it all.

Henri, a dapper Frenchman and most discreet of servants, greeted them most effusively.

'*Bon jour, Monsieur. Bon jour, Madame.*'

A good many women had Monsieur brought here – each one his 'wife'. Henri cheerfully accepted them all. But he looked at Robin kindly. She seemed to him very young and very charming. She took Monsieur's arm and walked from room to room, in raptures over everything. She loved the drawing-room with its amber satin panelled walls and cunningly hidden lights. Here was a soft carpet into which one's feet sank; exquisite painted furniture; a baby grand piano which Aubrey played. He promised to play after dinner.

There were two bedrooms. One which Aubrey called his

dressing-room. The other seemed to her much too effeminate to suit a man. It was the last word in luxury. Gold satin curtains; black carpet; a huge bed with a gilt back and a cunning little light fixed on to it. A semi-circular dressing-table of some satiny wood covered with gold and tortoiseshell requisites; crystal scent bottles, gold backed brushes – surely more suited to a woman than a man.

Aubrey picked up a tall bottle, pulled out the stopper and raised it to his nostrils.

'Ah!' he murmured. 'Lovely! Come and let me put some on you, my sweet. It's delicious stuff. It's called "*Ce soir ou jamais*".'

'My French is awful. What does it mean?' asked Robin.

'Never mind,' said Aubrey. 'Come here.'

He dabbed the scent behind her ears and on her throat. '*Tonight or never*,' he translated to himself.

'God, I love you,' he said aloud.

Robin's heart began to pound. Such ecstasy was almost pain.

'This looks very much like a girl's room, Aubrey,' she said as she took off her hat.

'I wired to Henri last night and he prepared it for you,' lied Aubrey smoothly.

How was she to know that she was only a successor of many others?

'If you don't mind, Aubrey, I shall go to bed soon after dinner and have a good night's rest,' she said. 'Otherwise I'll make a wretched sort of bride tomorrow.'

Aubrey did not look at her. He lit a cigarette and walked to the door. Robin was so very direct and simple. Perhaps this wasn't going to be as easy as he had anticipated.

He was in a gay mood for the rest of the evening and charming to her. Henri served up a delicious supper. There was champagne but Aubrey drank most of that. Robin assured him that wine went to her head so she barely tasted hers and nothing he said would dissuade her.

He began to see that this 'babe' had a will and a mind of

her own and while it increased his admiration it also re-
doubled his desire to master her.

After supper he made her lie on the sofa in front of the
electric fire. He played to her and Aubrey played well –
improvised – tunes of old songs. She watched him dreamily
through half-shut eyes and he saw by the rapt expression on
the pale young face that she was in that melting mood which
he needed. He seized his opportunity. He got up from the
piano stool, switched off the lights; knelt beside Robin and
slipped his arms beneath her. She could just see his face,
extraordinarily handsome in the flickering firelight.

His lips strayed to her ear.

'My sweet, how much do you love me?'

'Terribly. More than anything in the world.'

'So much that you would do anything on earth for me.'

'Yes, anything.'

'I might ask a lot.'

Something in those few words brought her from the clouds
of ecstasy to stern reality. Her large, grave eyes searched his
face.

'What do you mean, darling?' she asked.

He took the bull by the horns now.

'I mean – you won't send me away from you tonight, will
you, Robin?'

She lay very still against the cushions. She said very quietly,

'I think I understand, Aubrey. I know people don't attach
much importance to virginity nowadays. I don't want to seem
a sickening prude but I've got principles that I simply couldn't
break. To me, it would simply spoil everything if I slept with
you tonight.'

'Why should it?'

She put out a hand and touched his dark, shapely head with
a tender gesture which would have moved a man less callous
than Aubrey to pity and understanding.

'Try and see. I may seem a bore, but I've built up all sorts
of ideals and one of them was to keep myself absolutely pure
for my husband and that means tomorrow – not tonight.'

Aubrey felt suddenly furious – not with himself but with

26

her. He was disappointed and frustrated and not interested in her ideals.

But he was not yet ready to accept defeat. She was ravishingly pretty with her long slim legs and small waist and those large hazel eyes. He tried to be patient and began to reason with her on the subject of morality.

The front door bell rang.

Aubrey stood up and smoothed his hair.

'Damn,' he muttered. 'Now, who the hell is that?'

Robin also stood up. She felt nervous and unhappy. With all her heart she wished things had not turned out like this.

'It will be all right,' she told herself. 'Aubrey's okay, he'll see what I mean – he'll understand – I know!'

'I must answer that damn door,' said Aubrey. 'Henri's gone. He always goes at ten o'clock. It's half-past eleven.'

Robin raised her eyes to him. Her lower lip quivered nervously.

'I'd no idea it was so late, Aubrey. Who is it – do you expect anyone?'

'I don't know – I'll see,' he said.

He spoke ungraciously. Her resistance of him had ruffled his vanity and he felt impatient and irritable. He lit a cigarette and walked to the door and his expression was not good to see.

Robin stared after him. She heard voices in the hall. A moment later Aubrey put his head round the door. He looked flushed and bad-tempered.

'It's a pal of mine. Henry Rushton. Sickening nuisance, but I can't refuse to give him a drink. I'll explain about him later. You're my wife – don't forget it for lord's sake, Robin.'

She blushed scarlet.

A tall man entered the room, followed by Aubrey.

'Very decent of you to let me come in. I know it's frightfully late,' he was saying.

Then he saw Robin and stopped. He looked amazed – and, so Robin imagined – amused.

'I beg your pardon,' he murmured. 'I had no idea –'

'Oh, that's all right, Rushton, my wife,' said Aubrey casually, indicating Robin. 'Robin darling – an old pal of mine.'

Henry Rushton bowed.

'How-do-you-do,' he said stiffly.

'How – how-do-you-do,' said Robin, stammering, fiery red, and put both hands to her heart, wishing that it would not pound so hard. She had never felt more embarrassed and wretched in her life.

'So you've been abroad all this time, Henry?' said Aubrey, handing him a cigarette. 'Sit down – have a whisky.'

'Perhaps – a weak one,' said Rushton. He was still eyeing Robin. He guessed that she wasn't Aubrey's real wife. Aubrey had just grimaced at him – a significant wink. Rushton was, himself, a quiet and temperate man whose hobby was collecting antique jewellery which he bought and sold as the fancy took him. He was over forty – a man with set ideas; a rather cold nature. He disliked women and mistrusted them.

Henry, with his austerity and conventionalism, bored Aubrey, but Henry knew a lot of rich, influential people and Aubrey considered it a good thing to keep in with him. One never knew when one needed a worthy, influential friend. From Henry's point of view Aubrey was not altogether to be despised because he travelled widely and on many occasions had picked up a good stone for the quite famous Rushton collection.

Rushton thought Robin rather pretty and much too young.

'What a shocker Aubrey Mauldron is,' he mused. 'But she's probably as bad as he is. These innocent looking girls are often the worst and if she wasn't that sort she wouldn't be here like this.'

He seated himself comfortably, took the drink Aubrey handed him and explained his late visit.

'I only arrived in Paris half an hour ago – back from Rome. I met Henri walking down the road outside my hotel and he told me you were back in Paris, so I thought I'd look you up. But, of course, I didn't realise you were – er – not alone.'

'Quite all right,' said Aubrey. 'Delighted, and so's Robin. Well – how's Rome? I am very fond of Rome. Best night clubs in Europe.' He laughed although the other man looked disapproving.

As the two men began to talk Robin sat on the edge of the sofa, looking and feeling embarrassed. She wondered why this man, Henry Rushton, didn't congratulate Aubrey on his marriage and why they both ignored her in this rude fashion. For the next half hour they talked without ceasing and she might not have existed. Gradually the colour faded from her face and she began to look white and tired. And after another quarter of an hour, she rose and announced that she was going to bed.

The two men stood up.

'I must be going myself,' murmured Henry.

'Oh, don't hurry,' said Aubrey. He thought: 'I'll teach little Robin a lesson. It doesn't do to let the girls think you're too keen. . . .'

'Good night,' said Robin, raising her eyes to Henry Rushton.

She met his cool disinterested gaze.

'Good night,' he said.

'Later, darling,' said Aubrey carelessly.

Robin fled from the room and shut herself in her bedroom. And suddenly, without knowing why, she turned the key in the lock. Then she sat down on the edge of the big, luxurious bed and hid her face in her hands.

Why, why had that hateful, superior man come and spoiled everything? And why did Aubrey treat her so casually in front of him? She felt cheapened; humiliated. She didn't know why. She wished that she had not come to Aubrey's flat tonight.

Then she looked toward the door. The handle was being turned. She heard Aubrey's gay voice.

'Darling . . . Robin . . . are you there, sweet?'

She walked to the door, deciding not to be a fool. She opened the door. She stood quietly facing Aubrey. He had had more to drink and was flushed and amiable again.

29

'My darling,' he said, taking her in his arms. 'I'm so sorry that fellow turned up. He's just gone. Bores me to tears, but we've known each other for ages. I had to ask him in for a drink – hadn't I?'

'Of course,' she said and hid her face against his shoulder and clung to him for a moment.

He stroked her hair.

'Tired?'

'Yes. I'm going to bed now. Aubrey – does that Henry Rushton really think I'm your wife?'

'Of course. It doesn't matter anyhow.'

'No, I suppose not.'

'Let me brush your hair for you, Blackbird.'

'That's a new name,' she said, trembling between tears and laughter.

'Robin or Blackbird – both charming,' he said in his facile way. 'You've got a little black head. I want to brush your hair for you. Slip into your dressing-gown.'

Then, very white, very bright-eyed, Robin drew away from his arms; smiled at him and shook her head.

'No, forgive me, darling. I'm awfully tired. I'm going to kiss you good night. We'll have breakfast together.'

A moment's silence. Aubrey Mauldron was as white as she was, and there was a hardness about his lips and in the eyes that frightened her. Then he laughed.

'Don't be a little idiot, sweetheart.'

Deliberately she stood on tip-toe and brushed his lips with hers.

'Good night, dear.'

'No, by God, no,' he said, and caught her against him.

Just for a moment she was quiescent; shivering as he set his hot lips against her mouth. Then passion left her and she felt cold and hard. With a strength that surprised him, she pushed him away.

'Good night, Aubrey – *please*,' she said, panting.

Then the hot Irish temper flared up. He broke into a stream of furious, passionate words.

'Damned little prude!' he shouted at her. 'Good God, is

your love so poor that you've got to wait for a marriage contract and a ring on your finger? Old-fashioned drivel . . . sheer funk . . . I thought you were worth more than that . . . but I can see I ought to have left you in your "Rosary". . . . Ye gods . . . that's about where you belong if you're such a saint . . .'

'Stop, *Aubrey*!' Robin broke in, white-lipped. 'Oh, stop – please – *please*.'

He laughed – uncontrolled.

'I'm not going to marry you, if that's what you want – *I'm not going to marry you*. Do you hear me? I'm not a marrying man – so if you want to keep me as your lover you'd better get rid of these damned ideas and make yourself a little more pleasant. . . .'

She did not answer. She stood rigid and stared at him in stony silence.

The man's fury simmered down. He saw what he had done. He knew from the sick look in her eyes that he had lost her – lost something that he would never get back in this world. He cursed himself. His wretched temper! This wasn't the way to keep the love of a girl like Robin Frayne; neither had he gone the right way to make her forsake honour and principles for his sake.

He took a handkerchief from his pocket and wiped his forehead.

'I'm sorry,' said Aubrey, jerkily. 'Sorry, Robin. But you drove me mad – holding me off like that.'

Then she found speech. She was astonished that she could speak so quietly.

'Did you mean what you said to me just now?'

'What did I say?'

'That you – that you never intended to marry me?'

He moistened his lips and took a step toward her.

'Look here, darling – '

'Did you mean it?' she interrupted.

'In a way . . .'

'There can be only one way. Answer me – please. You

brought me here to Paris without any intention of marrying me?'

The hardness in the young voice made him curiously uneasy.

'Robin darling – ' he began.

'No,' she interrupted. 'Don't come near me. Don't touch me. I want the truth. Did you bring me to Paris in the belief that you'd just trick me into living with you – *living with you* – as your mistress – not your wife?' ,

'Don't put it like that,' he muttered, averting his gaze. 'Damn it all – people do these things – and –'

'I quite understand,' said Robin. 'You needn't go on. It was just a cheap trick – all that talk about marrying me. Oh, Aubrey, how you've hurt me . . . I loved you more than I've ever loved anybody in my life and I thought you were so wonderful.'

Even the simplicity of that could not break through the crust of Aubrey's selfishness and sensuality. He scowled at her.

'You aren't a bread-and-butter Victorian miss, Robin, damn it!'

'No,' she said. 'I'm not at all ignorant if that's what you mean. But if only you'd been honest with me.'

'What do you mean – honest?'

'I mean – if only you'd been decent enough to put things to me frankly . . . told me that you didn't want to marry me . . . '

'You wouldn't have come, would you?'

She looked him full in the eyes. Her face was burning now and her eyes full of tears.

'No. I don't think I would. But I'd have respected you for being honest and if we'd said goodbye then I'd have had something lovely to remember . . . your friendship . . . your kindness. Now I can only remember you with the utmost contempt.'

The handsome face of the man went scarlet.

'Damn it . . . '

'Don't go on saying "damn it",' she broke in wearily. 'I –

can't stand much more, Aubrey. Please leave the room. I'm going to . . . pack my things.'

'Robin, don't be absurd. . . . '

'Do you think I'd stay?' She swung round on him in sudden anger, her eyes blazing. 'Do you think I want to stay in this flat another hour after the way you've insulted me? I feel humiliated enough.'

'Robin – be sensible. I'm sorry if I lost my temper, and I admit now that I ought to have told you the truth in England, but I was so afraid of losing you. It was because I wanted you – honestly, darling – and I still do.'

'I don't doubt that,' she said with a frozen little smile. 'But wanting a woman and loving her are two different things – aren't they, Aubrey?'

'Robin, I'll be awfully good to you – '

'Thanks,' she broke in. 'Don't bother to go on. I'd rather go down on my knees and scrub floors than stay in this place and let you be "good to me". I'm sorry but I'm afraid I don't love you – I don't even like you. I think you're the most despicable man I've ever met. A common cheat . . . '

He went livid.

'All right. If that's how you feel about me, clear out.'

She turned to the bed, blindly, and began to pick up her things and put them in her suitcase. He watched her with bloodshot eyes.

Somehow or other her trembling hands managed to pack the suitcase and she put on her hat and coat. Then Aubrey crossed the room to her side. He was as white as she was, now.

'For God's sake be reasonable, Robin – you can't go out at this hour of night – you don't know Paris – it's ridiculous. Stay here. I won't touch you. I swear it.'

She brushed aside the hand he held out to her.

'I'm sorry. I don't believe a word you say. Goodbye.'

'Where are you going?'

'I don't know.

'You haven't any money.'

'If you try and give me any I'll throw it in your face.'

He looked after the proud young figure and knew then that he had lost an incomparable woman and that he admired her more than he had admired any girl he had known in his life.

'You ought to stay here until morning, anyhow,' he said sullenly as she walked into the hall. 'If anything happens to you . . .'

'Nothing can happen to hurt me more than you've hurt me tonight,' she said white-lipped. 'I trusted you.'

She shut the door of the flat quietly after her.

Robin Frayne walked into the streets of Paris at midnight, carrying her suitcase, and trying to hold her head up high. But now she had left Aubrey's flat, she was not so controlled or brave. The tears chased down her cheeks and she sobbed under her breath.

Where could she go ? What could she do ? She didn't know. Blinded by tears she walked on and wished terribly that she were dead. It was the end of everything for her – everything in the world.

Blindly, aimlessly Robin walked and walked until her body was one great ache of fatigue. Once a couple of harmless youths . . . students . . . spoke to her. She neither answered nor looked at them and they passed on, shrugging their shoulders. Once a bearded man came up and leered into her face and said,

'*Bon soir, Mademoiselle* . . .'

She woke up from her lethargy and said,

'No, no, please . . .' and hurried on.

She walked on, exhausted and hopeless. Finally she came to a big café, brilliantly lighted and crowded with people eating supper and drinking beer in long, slim glasses. There were chairs and tables on the pavement under a striped awning. It was not cold tonight and one or two couples were sitting outside.

Robin found a chair; sank into it and shut her eyes.

A grey-haired woman in evening dress and a fur coat, at the table beside her, glanced at the girl and then whispered in English to the man who sat with her,

34

'George, doesn't that poor girl look deadly ill. Is she ill, do you think?'

The man – unmistakably British and ex-Army, looked at Robin and pursed his lips.

'She certainly looks bad, poor thing.'

A waiter came up to Robin.

'*Bon soir, Mademoiselle . . .* '

Robin opened her eyes. The English couple watched her covertly and with curiosity. She put a hand to her head and said,

'Could I have some . . . water . . . I feel so . . . faint . . . '

Then the grey-haired woman stood up.

'George, she's English. And she's ill. I'm going to speak to her.'

'Do, my dear,' said her husband.

And that was how Robin came to meet the Williamsons in Paris, at the Café Mazarin, that unforgettable night.

Years later, Robin remembered the kindness and charity of the middle-aged couple who did so much for her at a moment when she was broken to pieces, mentally, and physically at the end of her tether. In whatever other way she had been unfortunate, she was at least lucky in her encounter with the Williamsons. Grace Williamson was what the world called a 'good woman' and with her, goodness and kindliness walked hand in hand. It was her *métier* in life to befriend the friendless and shepherd the lost lamb. She just couldn't help herself. She was that beautiful thing a born mother and she had lost her only child in an accident, a girl of twenty-two.

Williamson, a retired Colonel, was devoted to his wife and her word with him was law. When she returned from Robin's table and told him that she was going to take the girl back to their hotel for the night he didn't protest. Grace said the girl was all right, so she was all right.

'She's had a terrible shock – she's been frank with me and told me all about it and I think it's an absolute tragedy,' Mrs Williamson declared. 'And George, she has eyes exactly like our darling Betty's. I simply couldn't leave her alone like this in Paris. It's lucky we found her.'

35

'Lucky for her, *you*'ve found her, my dear,' said the Colonel.

But later when he saw Robin in a better light he knew that he would have helped her, if Grace had not. It was true. There was something in those soft hazel eyes of Robin's that reminded him of his idolised daughter.

So it was under the shelter of Grace Williamson's maternal wing that Robin crept from the storm that had broken over her head that night. And possibly it was Mrs. Williamson's kindness and understanding that saved her from utter despair.

'The man, whoever he is, isn't worth loving, my dear, so you must try and forget all about him and begin again,' Mrs. Williamson said to Robin again and again after she had helped her to bed and made her drink some hot soup in the hotel at which they were staying. 'Don't waste a tear on him. Just face life bravely and thank God nothing worse happened than this.'

Robin, infinitely thankful for the quiet room, the warm bed and the peace of it all after the havoc Aubrey had wrought, clung to the kind hand which Grace Williamson held out to her and wept bitterly.

'I loved him, Mrs. Williamson. I trusted him.'

The older woman looked at the bowed head.

She smoothed the dark hair back from the hot young brow and said,

'It isn't much use telling you so tonight, my dear, but the biggest consolation I can give you is to assure you that you'll get over it. You're young and you will.'

Robin raised a flushed, wet face.

'It isn't that I love him any more,' she whispered. 'I couldn't. He was too . . . too *beastly*. But I can't forget the awful humiliation of it. And that other man coming in – his friend – the shame of it – being told I was Aubrey's wife . . .'

'It was abominable,' said Mrs. Williamson. 'But I don't think any irreparable harm has been done. You'll never see either of them again.'

'I hope not,' said Robin, putting her face in her hands.

36

'What you must do is to stay here with us a day or two and we'll try and think out something for you . . . I know a great many people . . . I might get you a job somewhere.'

'Why should you trouble?' asked Robin chokily. 'You've been so kind . . .'

'Nonsense,' said Grace Williamson. 'Now drink up your soup and go to sleep and forget all about it.'

But long after Mrs. Williamson had gone and Robin was alone, she was awake. She could not sleep. And she knew that never, while life endured, would she ever forget.

CHAPTER IV

ABOUT three months later, Paris and all that had happened in Paris seemed a very long way away to Robin Frayne.

A perfect June morning found her sitting in the garden of a very charming house in Sussex, with a pile of mending – the very picture of peaceful domesticity.

This garden seemed to her an enchanted one; where anybody's dream might come true.

In front of her lay the house; sixteenth century, cunningly restored and in perfect repair, with the original mullioned windows; roof yellow with stone crop and seven tall Elizabethan chimney stacks, defying the ages and the elements.

Perfect peace reigned here. Robin could hear nothing but the twitter of birds; the occasional call of rooks in the tall trees; the hum of bees. Peace and plenty. And only twelve weeks ago she had been broken and swept by an acute emotional storm from which she had never thought to emerge whole again.

Fortunately for her she had been given neither time nor opportunity to remember Aubrey and that fantastic nightmare in Paris since she had been found and befriended by Grace Williamson.

She had only stayed in Paris one more day and then had returned to England with the Colonel and his wife and spent a week recuperating from shock in their flat in Hampstead.

Grace Williamson had fully understood the girl's disinclination to return to her sister in Shelbury. She had also satisfied herself that here was a fine, sensitive nature which wanted careful handling and proper environment.

The Williamsons could not keep Robin with them. They were going abroad to Canada to visit Colonel Williamson's married sister in Vancouver. Before they left, Mrs. Williamson heard from an old friend – Lady Quest who lived at Little Priory, which was the name of her famous old house in West Hamley, Sussex. Lady Quest wanted someone to help in the house, and to be company for her young daughter Nancy, convalescing from a serious illness.

'Do you know a nice girl . . . ?' Lady Quest had written to Mrs. Williamson, and Grace Williamson had looked at Robin Frayne and known that here was a nice girl.

So the Williamsons sailed for Canada and Robin found herself at Little Priory as a companion-help. And if it was more 'help' than companion, Robin did not mind. Passionately grateful for this chance, she threw herself wholeheartedly into her work. Lady Quest found that Grace had sent her a most industrious girl and that satisfied her.

Robin liked the Quests. Lady Quest was a rather vague, kindly woman, always occupied with deeds of good work in the locality: fêtes, bazaars, Women's Institute meetings and society calls. Sir James was an old man and not very strong. He spent most of his time trying new cures. Nancy was a casual, rather self-centred girl – still a child in her way, and got along quite well with Robin.

Last but not least in the household, there was the son and heir – Christopher Quest. Christopher was a Lieut.-Commander in the Navy, and for most part of the year, on the high seas. At this precise moment he was home on leave and had been since Robin Frayne came to live at Little Priory. He was a very charming, good-looking boy of twenty-five, with an engaging personality and sense of humour which made him popular with everybody. His mother literally adored him. He was on good terms with his father, and Nancy, whom he called his 'kid sister' treated him, when he was home, as a young god.

Sir James thought there was plenty of time yet for his son to choose a wife, but Lady Quest had a match-making eye on the girl who lived in a neighbouring big house. Doria Southway. The Southways were hunting people. Doria rode well to hounds; was extremely beautiful, and had liked

Christopher since they were small children together. Chris was fond of Doria and Lady Quest dwelt always on the hope and belief that they would one day 'fix things up'.

Robin, sitting at her mending, this warm June morning, was a little surprised when Christopher suddenly appeared on the scene and strolled across the lawn to the oak under which she was sitting. She had thought he was out with his mother in the car. He wore white flannels and carried a racket in his hand. Watching him walk toward her, she thought how essentially nice he was. She liked him immensely. He carried with him a breath of the sea . . . something clean, buoyant, delightful.

In a dream that Robin had dreamed long ago – before the nightmare of Aubrey Mauldron had clouded her existence – a man rather like Christopher Quest had figured. But that was long ago. These days, Robin was afraid of love – afraid of dreams. She had been so terribly disillusioned and hurt.

Yet somehow or other when Christopher Quest smiled and said, 'Hello. Busy?' she had to smile back. The young man found the dimples in her pale young face alluring. She was usually so quiet and sober.

'It's much too nice a day to waste on sewing,' said Christopher. 'Have a cigarette.'

'No thanks,' said Robin, and added mischievously, 'It's too nice a day to waste on smoking.'

'How severe is our Robin,' said Christopher, throwing himself down on the grass at her feet and lighting a cigarette for himself. 'She neither smokes nor drinks, neither has she any vices.'

Robin laughed.

'That's all you know.'

'Have you any? Tell me about them.'

He turned his head and looked up at her. She could not help thinking how nice his head was . . . with that stiff, goldenish hair shining in the sunlight. His grey eyes crinkled with laughter, searched her face.

'How pensive we are. Tell me about your hidden vices.'

'Don't be absurd, Christopher.'

'I'm not. But I'm bored.'

'Why?'

'Mama has taken Nancy into town to shop and Papa is having his daily massage and I'm knocking balls into the net alone. Get on a pair of shoes and come and play tennis with me.'

Robin smoothed a patch on Nancy's favourite pair of jeans and shook her head demurely.

'I'm not here to play tennis.'

'What are you here for?'

'To keep an eye on Nancy.'

'And didn't Mother say her darling boy, her naval hero, must be amused?'

Robin shook with laughter.

'No, she did not.'

'Then she was unkind. I now charge you with a new and solemn task. To amuse me until the high lords of the Admiralty order me back to my ship.'

'Certainly not,' said Robin. 'I never heard of such a thing.'

He hugged his knees and sighed.

'Cruel,' he said. 'You have a heart of stone.'

She bit her lip.

'H'm,' she said.

'Why that cryptic "H'm"?'

He looked at her again. She suddenly blushed.

'Come and play tennis,' he said. 'Mother won't mind if you do.'

She coloured again and kept silence. He thought,

'She's a shy mouse . . . and she always seems scared stiff when I talk to her. I wonder what her history is? I wonder what lies behind those grave hazel eyes. She has the longest eyelashes I've ever seen.'

'I must finish mending these jeans,' she murmured.

'They're finished.'

'No – really.'

Christopher suddenly turned round and put a hand over hers. What brown, thin fingers he had . . . hard and essentially masculine. She wondered, now, how she could ever have liked Aubrey's soft, white hands.

'Robina Frayne,' said Christopher. 'You're trying to choke me off. Why? Do you hate me?'

'Of course not.'

'Then why not play a set with me?'

'Because honestly I must do my work.'

'I'll tell Mama I made you abandon it.'

'No . . . please . . . '

'Do you like me, Robin?' he asked again.

'Yes.'

'How much?'

'Very much. . . . ' Her cheeks were burning: her pulses fluttering.

'Robin,' he said. 'Do you know that I'm falling in love with you – fast!'

'No – no – you mustn't.'

'Why not?'

'It's out of the question.'

'What is?'

'This – this sort of thing – between us.'

'Sorry,' said Christopher with an unsteady laugh. 'I don't agree. Last night when you danced with me I knew it – I knew I was falling in love.'

'But you mustn't,' she repeated in an agony of embarrassment.

'But I want to,' he said tenderly. And now he stood up; and lifted her on to her feet and put both arms around her. 'I can't help myself. Don't you understand? Mother's tried to "get me off" as they used to call it, with a good many girls. She's never succeeded for the simple reason that I have never felt the slightest emotion for any of 'em. But for you. Oh, little Robin, you don't know how differently I feel about you.'

She looked up at him mutely for a moment. The brown, boyish face was infinitely tender. But his arms, his hands about her were urgent, demanding.

'Oh, Christopher!' whispered Robin, and let her head fall weakly on his shoulder.

'Darling,' he said. 'Do you like me a little?'

'*Like you a little!*' She was on the verge of tears and she could not tell him what she felt.

'Robin,' said Christopher, and put a finger under her chin and lifted her face. 'Look at me.'

'Don't,' she whispered brokenly.

He saw tears on her thick lashes and caught her to him with a swift gesture of tenderness.

'Darling – don't cry. What is it? Have I upset you? Don't you want me to love you?'

'You don't understand,' she said. 'Chris – I – I – you don't know me – you don't know anything about me.'

'My dear, what is there to know?'

She was silent . . . fighting with herself. She knew she ought to tell Christopher about Aubrey and Paris . . . yet it was all over now and no harm had been done. Why drag up that ugly story? It would only distress him – even offend him. Why hurt herself and him unnecessarily? Wasn't it better to let sleeping dogs lie?

'You've been here three months, haven't you, Robin?' said Christopher. 'Long enough for us all to know you and love you. Listen, my dear. I adore you. I knew it last night and I know it still more this morning. I want you to marry me, Robin. Will you? Do you care enough for that, my dear?'

Her heart beat frantically and her arms went round his neck. For a reckless moment she clung to him.

'Oh, Chris, oh, my darling – I do love you!'

'Oh, my little heart,' he said huskily. 'My little heart's love!'

Then his lips were against her mouth.

'Oh, my darling, my darling Chris . . . I'll never, never love any man on earth again – but only you . . . '

And this time she knew that it was true and lasting and that she must shut her mind to the memory of Aubrey and wipe it from the slate for all time.

Christopher lifted his head. She opened her eyes and smiled at him. He was quite white. He bent and kissed the little mole on her arm which had so intrigued him.

'My dear,' he said in a shaken voice. 'My dear, you're most

intoxicating. I feel – well – lord knows what I feel. You go to my head – you darling thing.'

'And you to mine. Chris . . . Chris . . . '

'Sweetheart – it's the most sublime thing that's ever happened. I hoped I'd find someone like you but I didn't think I'd ever be lucky enough.'

'Dearest . . . !'

Her hands strayed to his head. She touched his lips and eyes with those swift gestures of the cool, pretty fingers which so enchanted him.

'Who taught you to love like that, Robin?' he whispered. 'Little witch – you're wonderful! And your dimples . . . oh, my darling . . . they're adorable!'

The fierce thrill of loving him – of being loved by him – suddenly died in her. The laughter left her eyes and her heart sank. Who had taught her to love like that? Oh, *God*, why couldn't she forget that other man she had been in love with . . . so experienced and subtle and so despicable.

Christopher, unconscious of her regrets and her secret bitterness in an hour which to him was perfect, smoothed her hair back from her flushed forehead, and said,

'How young you look, sweetheart. You look as young as Nancy. It's like baby-snatching – to ask you to marry me.'

She laughed despite herself.

'Chris – how absurd. You look young, too.'

'That's nice. We're a couple of infants and we'll grow up together. Robin, my little love, I've never loved any girl but you.'

She shut her eyes and pressed both her hands tightly against his warm, brown cheeks.

'Oh, my darling . . . '

'I'm glad,' he said. But he did not ask if she had ever cared for a man before and she was ashamed.

'Chris – what will your mother say? Chris – I *can't* marry you.'

'But you've got to, darling,' he said, smiling, and his arms held her very tightly and there was a tight, set line to his lips which defied her to argue with him.

'Lady Quest won't like it,' she said weakly.

'Mother will accept the wife I choose. And what's wrong with Robina Frayne and why shouldn't she make the most adorable Mrs. Christopher Quest?'

She swallowed hard and shook her head. How could any woman who loved him resist him?

'I'm nothing – nobody.'

'You have all the qualities I want in my wife.'

'I'm not good enough for you, Chris.'

'Oh, for God's sake don't say that.'

'Chris – you're angry!' she said aghast.

'Yes, when you say a thing like that. Is there any reason why you should say it? Why aren't you good enough? Because you haven't any money and you aren't in so-called Society? What do those things matter? You've never done anything wicked or shameful . . . there's no reason why you shouldn't marry me – is there?'

'No,' said Robin in a faint little voice.

Then his lips were hard upon hers again.

'Sweet, my sweet, you made me angry . . . I couldn't bear you to say you're not good enough when I adore you.'

Her arms were locked about his neck. She knew that this was the end . . . she couldn't fight him any more. Whatever happened, she must love him and go to him if he wanted her. And after all, there wasn't anything in her life to be ashamed of; only things to regret . . . and that must be her secret punishment. Christopher need never know.

CHAPTER V

A TALL, lanky girl in faded jeans and with an untidy head of reddish hair, raced over the lawn, followed by a Sealyham terrier, and came upon the astonishing sight of Robin in her brother's arms.

Nancy Quest stopped dead.

Christopher, keeping one arm about Robin's shoulders, held out a hand to his sister.

'Hello, Nance. Be the first to congratulate us. Robin's promised to marry me. Wish us luck.'

Nancy stared at him, then at Robin.

'Good lord!' she said rudely.

She looked what she felt. Dismayed.

'Wish us luck, Nance,' repeated Christopher.

'Oh, of course – good luck,' muttered Nancy and turned and fled. She wished to break the news at once to her mother.

Robin's face was scarlet. She drew away from Christopher's arm.

'I knew this would happen. Nancy doesn't like it. The others won't, either – '

'That doesn't matter to us, darling,' broke in Christopher, with that stubborn twist to his firm lips again. 'I tell you, I choose my own wife, and if the family aren't pleasant, then it'll mean a split.'

'Oh, Chris,' said Robin. 'That's just what I'm afraid of. I don't *want* you to quarrel with your people on my account.'

'Don't worry. Nancy's only a silly child. Mama will be different.'

Lady Quest was different. She was much too well-bred and charming to openly express her disapproval of her son's engagement. But to say that she was pleased about it would

46

be untrue. She liked Robina Frayne very much. Robina was a nice, quiet, well-mannered little thing; she was also pretty and seemed decently educated. They had all thought her quite a sweet person. Grace Williamson had seemed fond of her.

But Lady Quest had never for an instant supposed that Christopher would be seriously attracted. She was bitterly disappointed. She had so hoped to have Doria Southway for her daughter-in-law.

'It can't be helped,' she told Sir James, when she was dressing for dinner that same night. 'The harm's done now. I must try and accept it cheerfully, and Chris seems very much in love and very happy.'

'She is a nice, pretty little thing, after all, my love. It might have been a barmaid,' was Sir James's remark.

'Jimmy – what a dreadful idea!' protested Lady Quest.

'I quite like the child,' added Sir James. 'Not a man-chaser, anyhow.'

'Oh, no – I can't accuse her of having made a dead set at Chris,' sighed Lady Quest. 'It's just happened and I'll try and make the best of it for my darling boy's sake. But poor Doria. This will be a shock to her.'

That night a special family dinner was held at Little Priory to celebrate the engagement of Lieut.-Commander Christopher Quest and Robina Frayne.

Everybody was so nice to Robin that she could not be other than happy. Rapturously so. There seemed no likelihood of a 'split' in the family. The old Quests accepted her charmingly. Christopher was delighted. And if Nancy was a little gloomy and silent during the dinner, nobody noticed it.

After the meal the family sat in the drawing-room and talked. Robin sat on the sofa beside Christopher, holding fast to his hand and asked herself if it was all true. Was she really his promised wife – accepted by his family – sitting here with him, listening to the plans Lady Quest was making for the future? It was like a dream.

Christopher's mother was suggesting that the engagement should be publicly announced at once, and the wedding fixed for the Autumn. But Chris looked at Robin and said,

'If I have to join my ship next month and go to Malta for a couple of years, I shall marry Robin before I go and she can join me in Malta.'

Robin's fingers closed round his hand. But Lady Quest's heart sank a little. Such a speedy marriage. And they knew nothing about Robin really . . . but Chris must do as he wished, of course.

Nancy grew more and more depressed. If only Chris had chosen Doria. What did he see in Robin? She wasn't half as clever or lovely as Doria. Nancy walked to the window, flinging back her mane of reddish, untidy hair with an impatient gesture.

She saw a big yellow car turn in at the gates of the drive and roll towards the house.

'Hello,' she said, turning back to the family. 'We have a visitor.'

'Damn,' said Christopher.

'Darling!' protested his mother, smiling.

'I don't want any callers tonight,' he said.

'It can't be a caller. It's nine o'clock,' said Lady Quest.

'It's dear cousin Henry,' announced Nancy.

'Henry!' repeated Christopher. He stood up and searched for a cigarette. 'Oh lord. How dull. However, you've got to meet some of the relatives sooner or later, darling . . . ' he added, smiling at Robin. 'And here's one. Mother's sister's son. Very prosy and boring and too good to live.'

'Darling!' protested his mother again. 'Poor Henry's very nice.'

A tall, thin man with an austere face came into the room.

'Ah, how are you, Aunt Margaret,' he said, going straight to Lady Quest. 'I hope you don't mind me coming in at this hour. I'm driving through Sussex on my way to Devon and as I struck West Hamley at dinner time I thought I'd run in and see you.'

'But of course, my dear boy,' said Lady Quest. 'There's always a bed for you here. You'd better stay the night. Stay a few days.'

'I meant to put up at a hotel –'

'Certainly not, dear. Stay with us. We'll be delighted, and you've come on a most important evening. We're celebrating Chris's engagement.'

'Indeed? What a surprise!'

The man called Henry turned and looked round the room. His gaze rested on the slender, dark-haired girl in the greeny-blue dress, who was seated on the sofa beside Christopher. His expression altered and became at first astonished and then horrified.

Robin sat like a creature turned to stone. Every drop of blood seemed to drain from her face and leave it white. She stared back at him. And she knew that Christopher's cousin Henry was Henry Rushton – the man who had seen her in Aubrey Mauldron's flat three months ago. The man to whom she had been introduced *as Aubrey's wife*.

Lady Quest was chattering on eloquently about Chris's engagement and how pleased they all were – playing up nobly to her son. Christopher stood up, shook hands with his cousin, then turned to Robin.

'This is Henry, darling. Henry – this is your future cousin Robin. We won't introduce her formally as Miss Frayne.'

Somehow or other Robin gained her feet. But the room was spinning round her. She felt sick.

'I expect you're pretty surprised, Henry,' Christopher's happy voice cut across the silence.

'Very,' Henry managed to say.

Then Robin held out her hand.

'How-do-you-do,' she said in a desperate little voice.

'Cousin Henry,' put in Christopher, placing an arm around her. 'He looks very formidable, does old Henry, but he won't eat you, will you, old boy?'

Henry Rushton smiled frigidly. He kept his gaze on Robin. A dozen conflicting thoughts chased through his mind. Of course he knew beyond doubt that this was the girl he had met in Mauldron's flat in Paris. She hadn't been called Miss Frayne there. She had been introduced to him as Mrs. Mauldron. But obviously not his wife. What in heaven's name was a girl like that doing at Little Priory? How dared she get herself engaged to Christopher? No doubt she was after his money.

He read passionate appeal in her eyes . . . he saw from the whiteness of her cheeks and the trembling of her under-lip that she was frightened out of her life. But it was not those things that kept him from denouncing her there and then. He considered that he ought not do or say anything about this girl here and now, with young Nancy in the room.

'This is frightful,' he thought.

But aloud he said,

'How-do-you-do,' barely touched Robin's hand and turned away.

Robin closed her eyes. The room stopped spinning round her. She drew breath again. So he hadn't given her away. But would he – later? Was he only biding his time? She stared blindly at him. He had turned his back on her and was talking to Nancy.

'God,' she thought. 'God, why should this have happened?'

It was a cruel trick of Fate that he, of all men in the world, should be related to the Quests.

She knew, tonight, how very much Chris meant to her. Her love for Aubrey Mauldron had been the infatuation of a foolish girl. But her love for Christopher Quest was a real, sincere thing – something amounting to worship.

Raising her eyes she looked across the room at him. He caught her eye and smiled. It was the warm smile of a man who is utterly happy and in love. The passion in those grey eyes of his thrilled her from head to foot. But there could be no happiness for her tonight. Wretched, uncertain, she looked from Chris to Henry Rushton. Once more she met that cold, accusing look in which there was both recognition and surprise. She bowed her head, biting her lips to keep herself from crying out aloud.

'Where did you meet your – er fiancée, Chris?' Henry asked, very quietly.

Chris removed his gaze from Robin and smiled frankly and happily at Henry.

50

'She came here as companion-help, a few months ago, old man. Isn't she a darling?'

Rushton's lips twisted slightly.

'You know I never rave about women,' he said.

'More fool you,' said Chris laughing. 'I always thought women were wonderful. Now that I've met and become engaged to Robin, I think them divine.'

'Love-sick fool,' was Rushton's mental observation. At the same time his palish blue eyes regarded Chris with some pity.

'You have not told me how she came to be here, Chris,' he said to his cousin, eyeing him closely.

'It was through a friend of mother's – a Mrs Williamson – who met Robin in Paris.'

'Ah!' said Henry under his breath, and added to himself, 'I knew I was not mistaken.'

'Robin was on holiday over there, and wanting a job, when Mrs Williamson met her,' said Chris.

Henry smoked in silence for a moment. He wondered what Chris would say when he knew about Robin's 'holiday in Paris'. The little gold-digger, he thought. She had deceived them all very cleverly.

Henry's cynical, ruthless thoughts ran on and on. And all the while Robin sat on the sofa wondering how long she would be kept in suspense.

'I can't go to bed without seeing him,' she told herself desperately. 'I can't –'

Nancy yawned and came away from the window.

'I'm off to bed,' she announced. 'You coming Robin?'

'Not just yet,' said Robin.

'Well don't forget you're taking a riding lesson in the morning,' said Nancy. 'And the Southways are coming to lunch.'

'I won't forget,' said Robin, trying to smile naturally. 'I shan't lose my beauty sleep.'

It seemed to her an agonisingly long time before Sir James and Lady Quest retired. When at last they rose, Chris's mother approached Robin and embraced her quite tenderly.

'Good-night, my dear, and I hope you will always make my boy very happy,' she murmured.

Robin's beautiful eyes filled with tears. She clung to the gracious woman a moment, thanking her brokenly.

'I love him – you know I will always do my best,' she whispered.

Robin was left alone with the two men; the one she adored; the other who was her bitterest enemy.

She looked at Henry Rushton. His hard, inflexible face did not reassure her. Wretchedly nervy, she sprang to her feet.

'I think I'll go to bed and leave you two men to talk,' she said.

'Oh, don't go,' began Chris.

'I'm tired,' she said.

'All right.' He rose to his feet also. 'Then I'll see you to the foot of the stairs!'

With his boyish, delightful laugh, he tucked an arm through hers and walked with her to the door.

Henry Rushton's narrowed gaze followed the pair from the room.

'Poor Chris,' he thought with half-contemptuous pity. 'There's a shock waiting for him.'

At the foot of the wide, carved oak staircase, which was one of the oldest, most attractive parts of the house, Chris took Robin in his arms and bending his smooth, fair head, pressed a passionate kiss on her throat.

'Darling,' he murmured. 'Good night – oh, it's marvellous, my Robin, to know that you belong to me now – that one day you and I won't need to part – to bid each other – good night!'

'I love you, Chris,' she panted. 'Oh, promise me that whatever happens you will always love me!'

'Whatever happens,' he said, nodding. 'How could I help it? I believe in you and trust you, my dearest!'

Suddenly she broke loose from Chris's embrace.

'Wait a moment – I'll be back – I dropped my hanky on the sofa.'

He stood leaning against the banisters, waiting for her.

'My wonderful Robin,' he thought. 'I'm damned lucky that she cares as much as I do!'

Robin fled back to the drawing-room, deserted now save for Henry Rushton. Panting, she stood before him a moment.

'Mr. Rushton – listen,' she said in a low voice. 'I know you have recognised me – that it is you who saw me in Aubrey's flat that night. But I am not what you think – yes, yes, I know I was introduced to you as his wife – but I wasn't – I – oh, I can't explain now, Chris is waiting for me, only – '

'Hadn't you better go back to him?' broke in Rushton's thin, cool voice.

'Mr. Rushton, be kind, be merciful,' she gasped. 'I swear I'm absolutely innocent. But give me till tomorrow – let me see you – speak to you first, before you tell Chris.'

'Why should I?'

'Because I beg you to,' she said urgently. 'If you have any kindness, any generosity, please let me speak to you tomorrow before you give me away.'

He frowned and tapped the ash from his cigarette.

'Very well,' he said in an undertone. 'I'll say nothing tonight.'

'Oh, thank you!' she said, her face hot and flushed, her small hands clenched together. 'Will you be down in the garden, early, please, before breakfast?'

'Very well,' he said shortly.

She turned and walked back to her fiancé. She knew Henry Rushton would keep his word.

'Found your hanky, darling?' Chris asked her.

'Yes,' she lied.

And she loathed that small white lie, because she loved him – did not want to tell him even the smallest untruth.

She felt Chris's arms around her.

'Darling, good night – and sleep well!' he whispered as he kissed her.

She clung to him for a moment; then he released her, and she went slowly upstairs.

'My future wife,' was Chris's exultant thought as he

watched her go. 'Ah, it's good to be alive – to be in love –
with her!'

*　　*　　*

Morning came.

Robin had not slept at all. Tossing, turning, troubled in
her mind, she had not been able to get one wink of sleep. She
felt languid and depressed when she stole down to the garden
before breakfast to meet Henry Rushton.

He had kept his promise and risen early. He was walking
over the lawn by the oak. He stood still as Robin approached
him, his narrow face rigid and unbending.

'Thank you for giving me this much grace,' was Robin's
greeting, in a low voice.

'I said I would hear what you had to say,' Henry answered
stiffly.

'I only want to tell you – to swear to you that I was absolutely innocent over that Paris business,' she said.

Henry raised his eyebrows.

'That's hard for me to believe.'

Hot, shamed colour surged to her pale cheeks.

'Oh, I know appearances are against me. But I swear it
wasn't what you think. Listen – I'll tell you exactly how I
came to be in Aubrey Mauldron's flat –'

Quickly, breathlessly she blurted out her story; told him
of her going to Paris with Aubrey; of his deception; his
promise to marry her, then his attempt to make her remain
with him as his mistress.

'He made me keep quiet – made me call myself his wife
when you arrived that night,' added Robin, twisting and un-
twisting her slender hands. 'But I left the flat – soon after you
did – ran away. It is true – I swear it's true!'

The passionate young voice, ringing with sincerity, made
Henry Rushton frown, and hesitate to accuse her further.
Perhaps she was telling the truth.

'Don't you believe me?' Robin asked, agonised by the
expression on his face. 'Can't you be decent and give me the
benefit of the doubt? I did think Aubrey meant to marry me –

54

I swear it – and I left his flat without – without sleeping with him. I swear that, too – '

Her voice was unsteady and her face a scarlet flame.

Henry Rushton dug his hands into his coat pockets.

'I honestly do not know whether to believe you or not,' he said in his cold, hard voice. 'Appearances are, I must admit, against you. Mauldron was undoubtedly in love with you and it's difficult for me to believe that he – that you didn't spend the night at his flat,' he finished, spreading out his hands with a significant gesture.

Robin bit her lower lip till the blood came.

'It is true – I swear it,' she said. 'Mrs. Williamson – Lady Quest's friend – who befriended me in Paris that night, can prove that she found me in a café after midnight, where I had run away from Aubrey.'

Rushton twisted his moustache.

'Even presuming you did run away that night, what proof have you that you were not living with Mauldron, for some time before that?'

'I only went away with him that morning.'

'So you say.'

'Oh, how can I make you believe me?' cried Robin in despair. 'Why are you so dead against me?'

'Because Chris is my first cousin, in the Navy, and the heir to a fine old title,' he said, with a haughty tilt of the head. 'There has never been anything questionable in our family – I do not intend to see Chris make a fool of himself.'

Robin winced.

'I love Chris,' she said. 'I know I'm not good enough for him – but I love him.'

Rushton frowned.

'I think you ought to tell Chris about your affair in Paris, anyhow,' he said. 'Let him decide.'

Robin caught her breath. She went white.

'I daren't tell him,' she said. 'He might begin to lose faith in me, and that would be grossly unfair. Even if he decided to marry me in spite of his doubts, I couldn't bear it – couldn't bear there being a shadow between us.'

Despite his own suspicions, Henry Rushton liked those words, and his hard eyes softened a trifle as he looked down at the girl.

'Look here,' he said curtly. 'I don't want to come between you and Chris if you are innocent – if that affair in Paris was merely the outcome of a stupid infatuation which harmed nobody. But I must have Aubrey Mauldron's word for that. If he corroborates your story – all well and good – your engagement with Chris can stand, and I'll say nothing.'

Light sprang to Robin's eyes.

'You mean that? Then I can write to Aubrey and ask him –'

'I will write and ask him,' broke in Henry coldly. 'It is to me he must answer. And if he confirms my suspicions, I'm afraid I must ask you to terminate your engagement with my cousin. You need not tell him the truth: You can just break your engagement and go quietly away.'

Robin shivered there in the sunlight where she stood. She felt cold and wretched. What would Aubrey say in answer to Henry's questions? Would he be decent and honourable and defend her?

'If you don't mind, I'll go back to the house and write my letter to Mauldron at once,' said the unmoved voice of Henry Rushton. 'Until his reply comes, nothing more need be said between us.'

Robin bowed her head.

'Thank you,' she said in a low voice. 'And if Aubrey tells the truth I have nothing to fear.'

With an almost imperceptible shrug of his shoulders, Rushton left her.

* * * *

The rest of the day passed without event.

Henry Rushton avoided her as much as possible. When forced to speak to her he was studiously polite. Sir James and Lady Quest were very kind and charming and did everything possible to make Robin feel that they welcomed her and did not resent her engagement to their son.

The Southways lunched at Little Priory that day. Robin, with all humility, wondered every time she looked at Doria Southway, why Chris had not asked her to be his wife. She was a handsome girl – tall, fair, clever – a brilliant conversationalist – very modern – seemed very much at ease with Chris and used her sparkling blue eyes to advantage.

Robin felt dowdy, old-fashioned, and stupid, in comparison with Doria. Yet when Chris turned to her, his whole face changed.

Although, outwardly, Doria was perfectly friendly toward Robin, inwardly she seethed with jealousy and dislike of the girl Chris had chosen. Ever since she had known Chris she had been in love with him – and had hoped and believed that he would one day ask her to marry him.

'I won't let Robina Frayne have him – I want him myself –' she thought fiercely.

She would have given much to have known the agonising uncertainty of Robin Frayne's position as Chris's future wife – to have read what lay in Henry Rushton's mind.

And meanwhile poor Robin suffered and waited – happy only when she was alone with her fiancé, close in his arms, where she felt safe and protected by his love.

At the end of a week, her suspense with regard to Aubrey Mauldron's answer was ended – but in a manner calculated to send her further into the depths of despair.

Henry Rushton found her alone in the library, reading one evening just before dinner. The others had not yet come down. Robin's face flushed and she sprang to her feet when he entered the room, an opened letter in his hand.

'You – you've heard from – Aubrey?' she stammered.

'Yes,' he said. 'I have heard. He makes no statement – does not answer any of my questions. But he says he has been looking for you for weeks, and is coming over from Paris immediately, straight down to this address. This letter was written two days ago. That means that he may be here to see you at any moment.'

Robin put a hand up to her lips and a cry escaped her.

57

'No, no – he mustn't come here! Henry, you can't – you won't let him come – surely?'

Henry was quite unmoved.

'Why shouldn't I let him come, my good girl?' he asked in a tone that was undeniably insolent.

But Robin was beyond being proud just at that moment, and beyond caring whether Henry insulted her or otherwise.

With a feverish gesture she caught his arm with both hands.

'No, no – please, please stop him!' she panted. 'Henry. I'm not – what you think. I swear it! But Aubrey can't come here now – it – it would be an impossible situation!'

'It should never have been allowed to become possible,' said Henry Rushton. 'You had no right to accept Chris in the first place, knowing that you were Aubrey's –'

'No, no!' she interrupted, refusing to let him utter the name which she did not in any way deserve. 'You have no right to say that – to believe such a thing against me.'

'I tried not to believe it after our conversation the other morning,' he said. 'I decided to let Mauldron settle the matter for good and all. I wrote to him. I have told you his answer. He refused to answer my questions about your presence in his flat, and announced his intention of coming straight down to see you personally. Now I can and will do no more for you.'

Robin walked to the nearest chair, sat down and leaned her head against a cushion, gasping a little for breath.

'Henry, please,' she said. 'I can only assure you that I was quite innocent. I've said so many times, and you won't believe me' – her voice broke – 'but I swear it on my most sacred oath.'

'Then why didn't Mauldron admit that – leave you alone?'

'I don't know,' she said in a hollow tone. 'I can only suppose that he had some ulterior motive in wanting to come down here and torture me.'

'Of course,' said Rushton slowly, 'he may be coming personally to assure me of your – er – innocence.'

She caught at that like a drowning person at a straw.

'Yes, yes, it may be that!' she said hopefully. 'Oh, it is that, of course. It must be. Because Aubrey knows I was not to blame for – that night in Paris.'

'In which case, of course, I shall be ready and willing to apologise to you,' added Rushton, his voice and manner as chilly and distant as ever.

Robin drew a slender hand across her brow.

'I don't want you to apologise,' she said in a low tone. 'I realise that you've had cause to be suspicious. I only want peace – and the right to enjoy my happiness with the man I love.'

'At any rate, whether you lived with him or not, I am afraid I cannot prevent Mauldron coming here if he wishes to see you,' Henry went on. 'He will have to be introduced to the family as an old friend of mine and – yours.'

'He is no friend of mine,' whispered Robin. 'I never want to see him again. I loathe the memory of him.'

Rushton shrugged his shoulders.

'I am sorry. But if he comes, he comes.'

'Unless he has some particular wish to ruin my happiness, he will tell the truth,' said Robin. 'Then perhaps you will leave me alone – all of you.'

Henry reddened. Somehow Robin made him feel ashamed of himself, and he resented the feeling. He was about to make some sharp remark, when the library door opened and Chris came in, buoyant, youthful, delightful to look upon with his brown, handsome face glowing.

'Hullo, Robin darling! Hullo, Henry – how goes it?' he said cheerfully.

He was at her side before she had time to rise and greet him, sitting on the edge of her chair, putting an arm around her shoulders.

'Sweetheart, you look pale. Not ill, are you?' he said, with a note of concern in his deep voice.

A sudden wave of resentment against Henry for hurting and terrifying her, swept over Robin.

'No, I'm not ill, Chris darling,' she said in a loud, clear voice. 'Nothing wrong with me. I've just been having a – a sort of political argument with Henry.'

'Henry likes an argument, don't you?' laughed Chris, looking at his cousin humorously. 'And what do you think of my Robin's power of reasoning, eh? I can't argue with her for long. She's far more intelligent than I am.'

'Oh, my dear,' murmured Robin, leaning against him with a deep sigh which was stifled against his sleeve.

Henry, who considered any public show of affection embarrassing, turned his back on the pair and moved toward the library door.

'Oh, most intelligent – very clever, I should say,' he remarked.

The sneer in that observation was lost on Chris, but Robin winced under it. When the door closed on Henry, she turned to her fiancé with a little gesture of abandon, flinging her slim arms about his neck.

'Chris, Chris, I love you so!' she said in a smothered voice. 'Oh, my dear, I'd die if your love was taken from me now.'

His handsome, laughing face grew serious at once. He drew her into his arms, bending his fair head to kiss her.

'Dearest, why should my love be taken from you? It can't be when I adore you and worship you!'

Her eyes, full of grief, looked beyond him to the closed door through which Henry Rushton had just passed.

'No, perhaps not,' she said. 'But sometimes I'm afraid –'

'You need never be afraid of that. I shall love you all my life, Robin,' said Chris, in an earnest voice.

She clung to him speechlessly for a few moments.

The library door burst open. Nancy came in – saw them in each other's arms – and marched out again, banging the door behind her, a look of disgust on her tanned, boyish face.

Lady Quest, crossing the lounge, was nearly knocked over by her tall, youthful daughter; reproached her for not walking in a more 'ladylike' manner, then noted the look of disgust on her face.

'What's the matter, my dear?' she said, smiling.

Nancy hunched her shoulders and then nodded in the direction of the library.

'Chris and his dear Robin are in there, necking,' she said.

'It makes me sick to think that our Chris should be making such an idiot of himself over that girl. Why couldn't he have married Doria?'

'My dear!' protested Lady Quest, and her beautiful face in its frame of white hair, looked pained 'You really must try to think more kindly of Chris's engagement. We are all – er – disappointed about Doria – but we are trying to welcome poor little Robin with open minds and hearts and you must do the same.

'M'm,' said Nancy, scowling. 'Well, we none of us know anything about Robin's people or past, remember, Mater.'

Lady Quest passed into the library, her gentle heart and generous mind considerably troubled by her young daughter's words.

Somehow she did wish they knew a little more about dear Robin.

CHAPTER VI

ROBIN did not see Chris alone again that evening. Dinner over, Doria Southway arrived, and soon afterwards the Flemmings – great friends of both the Quests and the Southways. They had only been married a year and were still frankly lovers. Robin thought them a charming couple.

Neither Hugh Flemming nor his wife seemed able to enjoy life separated for more than a few moments at a time. Robin watched them with a tremendous feeling of envy. How happy they were – adoring each other – husband and wife!

'The Flemmings are a marvellous pair – as unashamed about their love for each other as they can be,' Chris whispered to Robin earlier in the evening. 'We'll be like that when we're married, won't we, sweetheart?'

Robin smiled and nodded. But later, while she sat beside Lady Quest, watching Chris dance with Doria Southway, and Hugh Flemming, quite unfashionably enjoy a waltz with his pretty, dark wife, she felt strangely depressed and anxious.

Chris, in the highest of spirits, finished the waltz with Doria, then piloted her out into the moonlit garden for a breath of air. He would far rather be out here with Robin, but seeing that she was about to dance with Captain Flemming, he took Doria for a walk.

'Awfully hot in that room tonight,' he remarked, as he walked down the path, mopping his face with a handkerchief.

'Yes – much too warm,' Doria agreed.

Her heart was beating fast, and her cheeks were a delicate pink.

'It's good to have you alone a bit, Chris,' she said, trying to speak lightly. 'I never see anything of you these days, and we used to be such good friends before you went to sea.'

Quite oblivious of her secret passion for him, Chris turned to her with his friendly smile.

'We did, and we still are good friends I hope Doria,' he said.

'Oh, of course,' she murmured, 'but now that you're engaged – ' she finished with an expressive shrug of the shoulders.

'My engagement to Robin doesn't spoil my friendship with you or anybody else,' he observed. 'Robin isn't like that – she would hate me to give up my friends because of her, bless her.'

His tender tone when speaking of Robin made Doria clench her hands.

'Let's sit down here a moment and have a smoke, shall we?' Chris went on, as they came to a rustic seat at the end of the rose-walk.

She tried to conquer the rising emotion in her, and sat down beside him. It was a charming part of the garden, hidden from the house by twelve tall cypress trees. Just in front of the seat, a marble faun, with a grinning, enigmatical face, stood on a square piece of lawn. The statue looked life-like in the white moonlight. Chris regarded it with humorous eyes.

'I remember playing round that faun when I was a little boy,' he murmured, as he lit a cigarette for Doria. 'Cunning looking little beast, isn't he?'

'Yes,' she said. 'Isn't he.' Then, 'Chris – I suppose you're very happy about your engagement?'

He turned surprised grey eyes upon her.

'Of course, Doria. Tremendously.'

She swallowed hard. The colour left her cheeks.

'Why, Doria – what's the matter?' he asked kindly. 'Anything wrong, my dear? Are you upset about something? You can confide in me like a brother, you know!'

'Yes – I am "upset about something",' she breathed. 'But I can't confide in you, Chris.'

'Why not, Doria?' he asked. 'I never dreamed you had any

sort of trouble. Tell me all about it and if I can do anything –'

'You could do everything,' she finished in a tense voice. 'But I can't confide in you, Chris. You would despise me – never understand – what your engagement meant to me. Oh, what am I saying? I must be mad!' she added, breaking off with a dramatic gesture, and an immense amount of feeling in her voice. Doria Southway was a born actress.

She covered her face with both her hands. And Christopher Quest stared at her bent, golden head, his good-looking face serious, his eyes very distressed – and surprised.

Awkwardly he touched that bowed, beautiful head.

'Doria – my dear – I'm so sorry – but I – don't know that I understand,' he stammered.

She knew that he did. But she took her cue from him. Raising her head she looked at him; tears on her thick lashes and sparkling very effectively in her blue eyes.

'No, no, of course not; let us go back. I – I'm being a fool. Give me another cigarette,' she said hurriedly.

Gladly enough he lit a cigarette for her. He was rather silent as he walked back with her to the house. But she had done all that she intended to do – let him guess that she was in love with him, and she knew he would not forget it.

Just before they reached the house, Doria paused and held out a hand. Her face was delicate, tear-stained, appealing.

'I – I'm just going to wander for a walk by myself. I'll be in in a moment. Don't take any notice of me, Chris. See you later,' she murmured.

'Always remember I'm your friend, Doria,' he said kindly.

She turned from him and walked down the path toward the drive, which led out on to the main road to Horsham.

As she approached the entrance to the drive, she was suddenly half blinded by two dazzling headlamps from an approaching car. She sprang to one side of the roadway, and the lights were thrown full upon her, showing up her tall, fine figure in the yellow dress. The car stopped and the driver got out and approached Doria.

'Pardon me, but is this Little Priory?' he asked.

Doria saw by the headlights that the stranger was good-looking and smartly dressed. She had never seen him in this part of the country before.

'Yes. These are the gardens of Little Priory. Sir James and Lady Quest live here,' she said. 'Can I help you – ?'

'Oh, thanks very much,' said the man. 'I've come to see a Miss – er – Frayne.'

Doria pricked up her ears. Chris's fiancée! Was this man a relation of Robin's? Or an old admirer?

'Miss Frayne lives here, too, yes,' she nodded. 'The whole family are up at the house, dancing. I'm Doria Southway – a guest of the evening. I've just come out for some fresh air. It's such a lovely evening, isn't it?'

'Marvellous,' he murmured. 'Allow me to drive you back to the house. It's only a little distance – but I'd be charmed.'

Doria smiled slowly and decided to take the offer. She seated herself daintily in the car, and the man took his place at the wheel. He liked pretty women, and he smiled agreeably at the golden-haired girl.

'Let me introduce myself,' he said. 'My name is Mauldron – Aubrey Mauldron.'

Doria made a mental note of the name.

'And you are a great friend of Robin Frayne?' she said sweetly.

'Quite an old friend,' said Aubrey, with his tongue in his cheek. 'Do you know Robin well?'

'She has just got engaged to my oldest friend – Christopher Quest,' said Doria, covertly watching beneath her long lashes.

'Ah,' said Aubrey, and she saw his eyes narrow.

'We're all very pleased about it,' purred Doria.

'When I heard about it, it was a distinct shock to me,' said Aubrey.

'Really?' said Doria very eagerly.

There was no time for further conversation between these two, who were equal in their capacity for cold, cruel selfishness and greedy passions. They had arrived at the house. But Doria had learnt a great deal in a few seconds.

'Come straight in,' she said to Aubrey. 'I will take you to Robin.'

'She may not expect me,' murmured Aubrey, removing his coat which he hung up in the hall. 'I drove down from town, and just had time to leave my luggage at the pub, and dash out here after a hurried dinner to see her for a few moments. I hope Sir James and Lady Quest won't mind –'

'I'm sure they'll be delighted to welcome a friend of Robin's,' said Doria, secretly enjoying herself.

Deliberately, she piloted Aubrey into the drawing-room. Without warning, she led him up to Robin, who was standing beside Chris, laughing up at him.

'A surprise for you, Robin,' said Doria in her sweetest voice. 'An old friend of yours – Aubrey Maudron – to see you!'

Aubrey's Irish blue eyes met those of the girl whose heart he had nearly broken, and he smiled, a slow, meaning smile that chilled her.

'My dear Robin!' he said in a theatrical voice, holding out both his hands. 'How wonderful to see you again!'

Robin wished heartily in that moment that the floor would open and swallow her up.

Aubrey seemed quite cool, quite happy.

'Simply wonderful to see you again,' he repeated, both hands still extended.

Robin pulled herself together with an enormous effort.

'I – what a – a surprise! – er – hello,' she stammered.

Doria had been watching Robin.

'It's perfectly obvious that she's taken aback by the appearance of this man, and that she didn't want to see him,' was her mental observation – drawn with such secret satisfaction. 'So far, so good. I must keep an eye on Miss Robin. I'm not at all sure she's the little angel Chris imagines!'

Aubrey took Robin's hand and pressed it warmly with both his.

'Dear little Robin,' he murmured. 'Just the same! You haven't altered a scrap. More beautiful than ever, perhaps!'

And he raised the ice-cold hand to his lips.

Lady Quest, regarding him from the other side of the room, pursed her lips and turned to Sir James.

'I don't think I like this young man, Jimmy,' she murmured *sotto-voce*; 'I never trust these hand-kissing fellows. He appears to be an old friend of Robin's from the way he speaks.'

Christopher looked at the sleek-headed man who was greeting his fiancée in such a familiar fashion, then at Robin.

'Won't you introduce me to your friend, darling?' he murmured, putting an arm about her shoulders.

The frozen look of fear, of repugnance, was still in Robin's eyes. The sight of Aubrey, the touch of his lips on her hand had shivered her with a thousand memories – memories of a past she had tried so hard to forget, but which now came sweeping back on her, almost choking her.

The room seemed to be suddenly hot and stifling. Suffocated, she put a hand to her brow and found it damp.

'This is ghastly,' she thought. 'I must pull myself together – '

'Robin, dearest, aren't you well?' she heard Chris's anxious voice, and, turning, looked into the grey eyes which could thrill her so completely. But she felt no thrill in that instant – only regret that Aubrey Mauldron had once occupied his place.

She smiled – a smile that would have wrung Chris's heart could he have guessed how much it cost her.

'Quite well – only the room is – so warm. Yes, of course, let me introduce – an old friend of mine. Aubrey Mauldron.'

'How-do-you-do,' said Chris courteously, holding out a hand. 'Any friend of Robin's is welcome to Little Priory.'

'This is my fiancé – Christopher Quest,' added Robin, her eyes upon Aubrey.

Aubrey looked down into those exquisite eyes that had once fascinated him so, and which still seemed to him particularly alluring. He read all the agony of appeal in her gaze. She was engaged to this chap, Quest, and obviously wished him, Aubrey, to keep quiet about that night in Paris. He was not so sure he wanted to keep quiet. But for the moment he could not very well cause an upheaval, he reflected. So he shook Chris's hand warmly.

'Glad to meet you,' he murmured. 'Hope you don't mind me coming at such a late hour, but I only arrived this evening, and felt I must come and see Robin before the night ended.'

'Delighted you came,' said Chris, in the same courteous fashion. Then to Robin: 'Introduce your friend to the Mater and Dad, won't you, sweetheart?'

She did so, moving now like an automaton, and feeling ice-cold. In desperation, she turned to Henry Rushton, who must know the torment of her mind.

'Please talk to him – tell him to go away,' she panted, in an undertone. 'You know him – you can send him away – I'll see him tomorrow – but not before all these people – I implore you – '

'Very well,' said Henry, taking care that nobody heard him. 'I'll see to it.'

She turned away from him, grateful beyond words.

'Good Lord, fancy meeting you down here, Mauldron!' he exclaimed, as he shook hands with Aubrey.

'Well, Rushton, how are you!' said Aubrey.

'Do you know each other?' asked Chris in a somewhat relieved voice.

'We were at school together,' said Aubrey.

'Mr. Mauldron is an old friend of Henry's – isn't that strange?' murmured Chris's mother, rather more happily, to Doria.

'M'm,' answered Doria, not at all sure she was pleased about this.

Chris was frankly glad to find the newcomer acquainted for so many years with his cousin. He could not honestly say he liked the look of Aubrey Mauldron. The man was rather too smooth for his liking.

Robin breathed more easily, and a little colour stole back into her white cheeks, as she stood there, watching Henry and Aubrey talk.

'I say, Mauldron,' Henry was saying, as he exchanged cigarettes with Aubrey, 'I think it's rather unfair of you to come upon Robin like this – suddenly, late at night, don't you know. I presume you have some definite reply to make to my letter, but I'd rather you came round in the morning to see her and me. This isn't the moment – '

'No, no, of course not, old boy,' finished Aubrey, easily, lighting his cigarette. 'I've no intention of making any scene. I've come, as you say, to reply definitely to your letter. Well, well! Who'd have dreamed Robin would come here and get herself engaged to your cousin?'

'It's all very awkward and I wish to goodness it had never happened,' said Henry angrily. 'But since I had seen her in your flat that night in Paris – ' He finished with a significant shrug of the shoulders.

Aubrey's brain worked quickly. He saw exactly what had happened.

His Irish blue eyes narrowed slightly and rested upon Robin. He had not seen her for months, but he had been haunted by the memory of her – had regretted allowing her to escape him.

To find her engaged to another man, and in love with that man; to meet coldness, repulsion from her, only fired him to greater desire for her.

'I won't stay more than a few moments, now,' he whispered to Henry. 'I'll just say a word to Robin, then be off. I'll get her to meet me in the morning.'

He moved to Robin's side.

'Why have you come?' she asked through stiff lips.

'To see you, my dear,' he answered.

'Why should you want to see me? When I left you in Paris, I left for good. I never meant to see you again.'

'But I meant that you should,' he said softly, looking deeply down into her face. 'Robin, believe me, I haven't known an hour's peace since you left.'

'You deserve no peace. You behaved like a beast,' she said, in a low, agitated voice. 'Oh, how dare you come down here like this – introduce yourself to the man I'm going to marry – his relations – his friends – ' She broke off, too agitated to continue, her cheeks scarlet.

And the man who had once loved her idly and lightly, realised in this moment that he wanted her now to madness.

'Don't waste time and words singing hymns of hate at me, my dear little Robin,' he said lightly. 'I have come down to see you for very strong reasons, and as for the man you're going to marry, well – '

'Well what?' She held her slim young body tense.

'We will discuss that tomorrow,' said Aubrey. 'The music is stopping, and your – er – dear Chris will be coming to claim you in a second. Listen, Robin – tomorrow morning at eleven o'clock – at the "Wheatsheaf" – half a mile from here, between this house and Horsham – you know it? Meet me there.'

'No,' began Robin in a fierce undertone.

But he interrupted.

'Yes. You can't refuse. And if you are not there, Robin – so much the worse for you!'

With that he moved away from her side to Henry Rushton and simultaneously, Chris, who had finished his dance with Joan Flemming, hurried across the room to Robin, eager to be with her for a few moments.

'Come out for a breath of fresh air in the garden,' he whispered.

In the fragrant hush of the garden, Christopher Quest put an arm around the girl he worshipped, and looked down at her face. It was pure and pale in the moonlight. He did not read the terror that lay in those beautiful eyes. He only thought how exquisite she was. He caught her close to him.

'My darling, my Robin,' he said in a low, passionate voice. 'I've wanted you so! It was horrid having to dance with Doria and Mrs. Flemming, and leave you to other men. I'd far rather have danced with you – just you – the whole evening. Oh, Robin, I think I shall carry you off tomorrow and marry you at once – I want you so much!'

'And I you,' she breathed, burying her face against his shoulder, and trying to restrain the wild tears that threatened to come. 'Chris, Chris, hold me closer – closer – never let me go!'

70

'I'll never let you go, little love,' he said, tightening his clasp of her. 'You're my whole world now. If it weren't that Mother and Dad will want a conventional wedding, I'd run away with you tomorrow – but I can't – for their sakes – we must do the thing properly – ' He broke off with a boyish, embarrassed laugh.

She nodded silently.

Christopher caressed the dark head that just reached his chin.

'Now, sweetheart, tell me about this fellow who was at school with old Henry. I've been aching to ask you about him. Felt quite jealous' – he laughed.

'You need not be,' said Robin, half closing her eyes. 'I – don't particularly like Aubrey Mauldron.'

'Aha! Disappointed suitor – pursuing my Robin and a bit sick because he finds her engaged to me, eh?' said Christopher. 'That's it, is it?'

She murmured a reply in the affirmative.

'I could never really be jealous of you, Robin,' Christopher said, after a pause. 'I trust you so implicitly.'

The hot colour swept across her face.

'I trust you,' she said in a stifled voice.

'I've never really loved any woman but you,' he said.

'If only I could tell him I've never loved any man but him,' thought poor Robin bitterly.

'We must go back to the others,' he whispered. 'But one more kiss before we go – and tell me again that you love me sweet – sweetheart!'

CHAPTER VII

ROBIN slept little that night. She was in a state of mind of inner turmoil, chafing against the necessity of obeying Aubrey, and meeting him next morning.

When the morning came, she managed to excuse herself from the family circle, and make her way out to the 'Wheat-sheaf' alone. Chris had, of course, wanted to come with her, but she had hinted that she wanted to shop in the village by herself and buy 'a secret' for him, so he had let her go.

She met Henry Rushton in the grounds on her way out.

'I am going to meet Aubrey at the "Wheatsheaf",' she said, her small face pale and set. 'In ten minutes time I should like you to join us there and Aubrey shall tell you the truth.'

Henry, sick of the whole affair, gave her a curt reply, promising to be there.

Robin walked on to the public-house where Aubrey awaited her. His magnificent car stood outside the little ivy-covered inn.

She felt cold and nervy when she finally faced him in a stuffy little bar-parlour, which smelt of stale beer.

'Now I am here, hurry up and tell me why you want to see me,' she said curtly.

'My dear girl,' he said, in the lazy voice which held a caressing note painfully familiar to her, 'don't look at me as though you could kill me.'

'I could – willingly,' broke from Robin. 'I loathe and despise you!'

'Oh, come,' he said, drawing nearer her. 'I'm not going to stand for that. Once you loved me – very much, too, as I remember! D'you think I've forgotten how you used to kiss me and want my kisses?'

72

Her face flushed scarlet.

'Yes – you can remember that – and humiliate me by the memory,' she said, nodding, a note of indescribable bitterness in her sweet voice. 'But it doesn't alter facts. I hate you now, Aubrey, as much as I cared. You killed my love. You took me away, swearing to protect me, to marry me, and then you tried to – to – oh – ' She broke off, burying her face in her hands. 'You were beastly – vile!' she added in stifled tones.

'Look here, Robin, I'm sorry about Paris,' he said. 'I admit I behaved badly.'

She raised her head – hope darting to her eyes.

'You admit it?'

'Yes. I'm sorry I didn't marry you, Robin.'

'It is too late to be sorry about that now. But if you see the wrong you did me, you can make amends now.'

'Yes, I can, and will,' he said, eyeing her oddly, and folding his arms on his chest.

'You mean that? You'll tell Henry Rushton that I was tricked into calling myself your wife that night?' She spoke eagerly, 'Oh, Aubrey, if you'll do that, I'll be grateful to you all my life.'

His eyes narrowed to slits.

'You are so crazy about this fellow, Quest, that you'd give anything to boot me off and marry him in peace, eh?'

She thought he was being sympathetic and understanding, and meant to do the right thing. A warm rush of gratitude, of relief, brought the tears to her eyes.

'Yes, I love Christopher Quest – with all my heart and soul, Aubrey. And Chris loves me as much as I love him. There is nothing between us except the shadow of that night in Paris, and Henry Rushton's suspicions. If you will tell him the truth, he'll keep quiet and leave me alone, and I shall be happy – absolutely happy, Aubrey.'

Her admission of genuine love for Christopher secretly infuriated Aubrey.

'Listen, Robin,' he said. 'I have said I'll make amends for what happened in Paris, and I will – '

'You'll tell Henry when he comes – ' began Robin eagerly.

'That I am willing to marry you, yes,' said Aubrey.

She shrank back from him. Her eyes gleamed with anger.

'You must be mad, Aubrey,' she said. 'How dare you suggest marriage to me now – after all that has happened? I'm engaged to Christopher Quest. I love Chris – worship him – I shall never marry any other man.'

Aubrey's lips curled disdainfully.

'Spare me your rhapsodies on Quest!' he drawled. 'They rather bore me, Robin, since I happen to be in love with you, myself.'

'In love! You don't know the meaning of the word! You degrade it!' she said passionately. 'Let me go! Let go of my arms at once!'

His eyes darkened.

'You aren't very affectionate these days, my little Blackbird,' he said. 'However, perhaps when we're married, you'll curb that nasty little temper you've so recently developed, and be as charming as you used to be.'

'No,' she said, struggling violently to release herself. 'I can never feel anything but hatred and contempt for you. And I shall never, never marry you!'

He suddenly let her go.

'Now listen, Robin,' he said in a quiet voice. 'It's no use struggling and quarrelling in a vulgar fashion like this. Let's discuss things sensibly.'

'I wish to discuss things sensibly,' she said, trying to speak with equal calm, though her heart beat at a suffocating speed. 'But, if you try to touch me again, Aubrey, I shall walk out of this place.'

He put his tongue in his cheek.

'We won't analyse your feelings toward me,' he said with assumed lightness. 'We'll just take facts. I am willing to marry you, and I shall tell Henry Rushton so.'

'But I'm not willing to marry you. Oh, can't you understand plain English?' she cried. 'I love Christopher Quest, and I am going to marry him.'

'Once you loved me. Does he know that?'

Robin looked white and unhappy.

'No – he doesn't know.'

'You haven't dared to tell him, eh?'

'I've nothing to be ashamed of,' she said. 'But I haven't dared to tell him – you're right – because he could so easily misconstrue my presence in your flat that night.'

'Just as Rushton misconstrued it?'

'Exactly.'

'Therefore, it stands to reason that your – er – dear Chris would not marry you if he knew that you had been in my flat in Paris.'

'Probably not,' she said, in a low voice. 'But even if he did marry me – he would have a doubt at the back of his mind unless you – you did the right thing and –'

'Cleared your fair name and took the blame?'

'Yes.'

Aubrey gave a hard little laugh.

'Aubrey,' she said huskily, 'won't you be decent and go away and leave me alone – leave me to marry the man I love, in peace?'

'I have nothing more to say except that I love you, and I am quite willing to marry you, myself, in order to get you.'

'If you loved me you'd go away – you wouldn't torture me like this.'

'Sorry,' he said. 'I want you. What I want I usually get.'

'I shall never, never marry you.'

'Very well. As you like,' he said, shrugging his shoulders. 'But when Rushton turns up I shall tell him I am willing to marry you, myself.'

She stared at him with frightened eyes.

'But don't you see what that implies – what Mr. Rushton will think?'

'Yes, I see.'

'He'll draw the wrong conclusions,' said Robin, feverishly. 'He'll think – oh – !' She broke off with a sharp little cry, and her face flamed again. 'It isn't fair – you can't let him think such a thing!' she added in a choked voice.

Just for a moment as he looked at her, Aubrey Mauldron

softened – felt ashamed of the way he was treating this girl. But the soft feeling speedily passed.

He put an arm around her.

'I love you – I want you!' he muttered. 'I won't give you up – no, I won't go away. It's no use asking me to.'

Robin felt defeated.

Shuddering, she drew away from his arm.

'Oh, what am I to do,' she whispered. 'Why are such men as you allowed to live?'

'You can make your own arrangements, Robin,' he said. 'I will marry you when and where you wish. The sooner you leave Sussex the better.'

She did not answer. She saw a car draw up and Henry Rushton's familiar figure step out of it.

'Henry has come,' she said drearily.

Henry Rushton came into the room, looking bored and disdainful. Closing the door behind him, he looked from Aubrey Mauldron to the girl whose slim figure was drooping, crestfallen.

'Well,' he said. 'Have you two finished your conversation? If so, I'd just like to hear the truth and be done with it. I'm rather tired of the whole affair.'

Robin swallowed hard – looked at him with tragic eyes.

'You won't believe me,' she said, 'but it happened the way I told you, and – this man refuses to tell you the truth.'

Henry pursed his lips.

'Oh, come, Robin, I'm not a child to be stuffed up with stories of that kind,' he said. 'If the whole affair was quite innocent, Mauldron will tell me so. I'm really anxious to end the business which is most unpleasant. But it's my duty to the family, and particularly to my cousin, who is the future baronet, to ask Mauldron – about Paris.'

He paused and looked questioningly at Aubrey. The latter did not meet his gaze. He was staring hard at Robin. When he spoke, it was in a low, deliberate voice.

'I'd rather not bring up details of the past,' he said. 'All I can say is – as I have just told Robin – that I am ready to marry her any time she wishes.'

76

Dead silence. Henry Rushton was too well bred to show on his face the effect these words had upon him.

'I see,' he said. 'Well, it's quite conclusive, Mauldron.'

A terrible look crossed Robin's white face. She turned to Henry, and said in a tone of the most passionate resentment,

'He has no right to let you think such things of me. I'm innocent – I have every right to marry Chris!'

'I regret,' said Henry, coldly, 'that I can no longer believe what you say, nor look upon you as fit to be the future Lady Quest. I must ask you to terminate your engagement with my cousin, today.'

'No – no –' she began wildly.

'Please do,' broke in Henry, 'otherwise I shall be under the painful necessity of having to tell him the story of your association with Mauldron.'

'He wouldn't believe it. He loves me – trusts me – he'll take my word –'

'Against mine? When I was introduced to you in Paris – in that flat – and told that you were Aubrey's wife?' said Henry, in the same icy tone.

'Oh, you will drive me mad between you!' cried Robin, covering her face with her hands.

'Take my advice, Robin, and don't make a fuss about this,' added Henry. 'It will only end in humiliation for you. I'm quite willing to say nothing to Chris about your past if you choose to break the engagement quietly. You can easily – er – suggest you have made a mistake, and leave Little Priory at once.'

'Made a mistake!' repeated Robin in a hollow tone, 'when I love him more than anyone on earth.'

'You can choose,' said Henry, moving uncomfortably. 'Either break the engagement and go – leaving him with – er – pleasant memories – or I shall be obliged to tell him the painful truth.'

'No – not the truth!' said Robin, looking at Aubrey bitterly. 'Lies – vile, cruel lies!'

He did not speak – only avoided her gaze. Henry Rushton moved toward the door.

'I leave it in your hands,' he said. 'If you have not broken your engagement with my cousin by tonight – I shall see that it is broken, myself.'

She did not answer. With eyes full of tragedy, she turned and walked out of the room.

CHAPTER VIII

ROBIN realised only when she reached home that she had not been to the village and bought a 'surprise present' for Christopher, which she had said she was going to do. But somehow, it did not seem to matter. Nothing mattered now. It was the end of all things, she thought wretchedly.

Henry Rushton had returned to Little Priory and he was the first person she met in the lounge.

'I've decided what to do,' she said in a low voice. 'I'll – speak to Chris tonight and break my – engagement – since I am being forced to do so. You'll – give me until tonight, won't you?'

Henry did not know why, but somehow the tragic misery in the girl's eyes worried him. He answered rather curtly,

'Yes, you may have until tonight. And please remember that it's your own folly that has brought this about.'

She did not reply to that. With a bitter little smile, she turned away from him. At that moment Christopher in spotless flannels and college blazer appeared, tying a silk scarf about his neck.

The sight of his handsome, cheery face made Robin feel suddenly sick.

'Why, hullo, darling!' he said. 'You back already? I thought you'd be much longer, so I've just arranged to play tennis at the Flemmings.' They rang up and asked me if I'd make a fourth.'

'Yes, of course – ' murmured Robin, trying to smile.

He saw that she was dead white and swaying a little on her feet. He rushed forward and caught her in his arms.

'Darling, are you ill? Are you going to faint?' he exclaimed.

'What's up? I've told the Mater several times these last two days, you're looking rotten!'

Robin pulled herself together with an effort.

'I'm quite all right, Chris. Stupid of me. I just felt giddy for a moment. The sun is very hot this morning. I didn't go to the shops, after all – turned back,' she said incoherently.

He smoothed the hair back from her forehead. His eyes were inexpressibly tender.

'My dearest – I can't have you getting sunstroke, or anything like that,' he said. 'Look here, I'll phone through to the Captain and tell him I'm not coming.'

'No – no – you must go, Chris – yes, please do, to please me,' she said. 'I'm perfectly all right now.'

'Are you certain?' he said anxiously.

'Positive.'

She smiled at him and squeezed his arm. Reassured, he dropped a swift kiss on her hair and let her go.

'Right you are, then, sweetheart. Go and lie down till lunch, will you?'

'Yes, I will.'

Henry Rushton, who had been standing by watching this little scene, his face wooden, asked himself whether Robina Frayne was to be pitied, or whether she was just a consummate actress. At any rate, he felt sorry for Chris – very sorry, he thought.

Robin, climbing wearily to her room, wondered what Chris would say when she told him tonight that she was leaving him, not for a short time, but for always.

She locked herself in her bedroom and lay down on the bed, having first drawn her blinds to shut out the brilliant sunshine.

Five minutes before luncheon she was still lying there on her bed, struggling for composure, wondering how to face what lay before her. She was roused by a violent banging on her door.

She started and sprang to her feet, pushed the damp, crushed hair from her tear-stained face, and walked to the door.

'Yes?' she said, in a calm voice. 'Who is it?'

'It's Nancy,' said a hoarse, frightened young voice, totally unlike the matter-of-fact voice of the normal Nancy. 'Oh, Robin, Robin, come quickly!'

'What on earth is the matter, child?' said Robin.

'An accident – an awful accident!' cried Nancy, breathing quickly. 'Chris – '

Robin flung open the door, forgetting her disordered appearance.

'Chris? An accident to Chris?' she said. 'What – what's happened, Nancy?'

'Henry – Henry went to the Flemmings' in Chris's car – to fetch Chris from tennis,' said Nancy, between convulsive sobs. 'You know Crayton Hill – that awful hill half-way from the Flemmings'? Well, something went wrong with the brakes and Henry lost control – '

'Yes, yes!' cried Robin as Nancy paused. 'Oh, what – what happened?'

'They crashed into a lorry,' continued the younger girl, hiding her face with her hands. 'Poor Henry was killed instantly, and Chris – oh,' she began to sob convulsively. 'They've taken him to the cottage hospital. Mother went with Dr. Oliver. Oh, Robin, I'm so afraid he'll die!'

'Die?' Robin clasped both hands over a heart that seemed to stop beating, then jerk on at a sick speed. Her face looked grey.

'Why wasn't I told before?' she asked in a low voice. 'I ought to have gone to the hospital too.'

Nancy ceased weeping, wiped her eyes, and looked through swollen, red-rimmed eyes at the other girl.

'Nobody knew where you were,' she said almost sullenly. 'Mother did ask. But what does it matter? What does anything matter if Chris dies?'

She spoke with the hysteria and pessimism of the very young who are faced with such grim horrors as sudden death. But those words, 'What does anything matter if Chris dies' – echoed and re-echoed in Robin's brain until they seemed to drive her mad.

The sound of a car was heard in the drive. Without another word she fled downstairs to the hall, careless of her tumbled hair and tear-stained face.

She reached the front door, flung it open, and was just in time to see the Quests' limousine drive up to the house.

The chauffeur, whose face was shocked and harassed, opened the door. The first person to step out was Christopher's mother.

Robin threw her an agonised glance.

'Chris – how's Chris – ?' was all she could say in a whisper to Lady Quest as she ran to her and gripped her hands.

'My poor Robin,' said Lady Quest, in a broken voice. 'This is terrible for you – as well as for us.'

'Chris – ' repeated the girl, with her heart in her mouth.

'He's alive,' said Christopher's mother.

'Oh, thank God!' said Robin.

'But very badly shaken,' added Lady Quest, and his left arm has a multiple fracture. It was a frightful smash. The car was wrecked. Poor Henry – ' She shuddered. 'It was useless. He was dead, and terribly crushed. They took him – away.'

Robin could not even begin to think about Henry or what his death might mean to her.

'I want to see Christopher.' She looked at Lady Quest with pleading eyes.

'You shall, my dear. They told me at the hospital that he may be brought home later today, provided I can get a trained nurse to look after him. I have already telephoned to a very good nurses' home in Brighton, and they are sending somebody at once. Dr. Oliver says he will have to be kept very quiet for several days.'

The gong sounded for luncheon, but nobody could pay much attention to the meal.

The hours dragged by until at last the ambulance bringing Christopher Quest home drew up at the door. Robin felt deathly sick as she watched the man she loved so desperately being carried in helpless on a stretcher. Could this be the gay, animated, laughing Christopher she had seen only this morning? She caught a fuller glimpse of his face as he was

carried by – such a white, piteous face, all the bright boyish-
ness gone, the lips twisted as though in pain. He had obviously
been given some drug, and his eyes seemed to stare at her
without recognition.

Sir James Quest, with Nancy hanging on to his arm, was
at the top of the landing, also watching Christopher being
carried to his room. The old baronet's face was pathetic. It
was his only son – his heir – who lay there looking as if he
were already dead.

Christopher was laid on his bed. The ambulance men tip-
toed out of the room, and Dr. Oliver bent over the insensible
form. Robin found herself staring at a closed door. She felt
horribly shut out.

'Chris!' she said aloud, in a queer, frightened little voice.

She felt Lady Quest's hand on her shoulder.

'Come, my dear – we mustn't stay here now. Dr. Oliver
will see to Chris.'

Robin turned and went with the older woman dumbly. The
look of suffering on her small, pale face, touched Christopher's mother. She patted Robin's head.

'There, my child, don't look like that. God has spared our
dear boy, and we must trust that he will soon be quite well
again.'

Robin pressed her hand convulsively.

'Oh, Lady Quest, I love him so – I can't bear it –'

'We both love him,' said Lady Quest, in her gentle voice.
'And we must both be brave, Robin.'

An hour after Christopher had been brought home,
Robin was still in the drawing-room, alone, walking up and
down, her cheeks colourless.

Through the open window she saw Nancy, and with her
Doria Southway, who had come to hear news of Chris. The
two were sitting on the lawn under the big cedar. Doria's arm
was around Nancy. They were obviously consoling each
other.

Then at last the drawing-room door opened and Lady
Quest came in. Her face was calm, as usual, although her
eyes were rimmed with red. Robin fancied she spoke more

coldly than usual and without any of the tenderness she had shown a few moments ago.

'Chris has asked for you,' she said, 'and Dr. Oliver thinks you had better go to him just for a second, Robin. No longer, mind you!'

Robin's heart leaped wildly. He was awake – he had asked for her.

'No hysteria, Robin,' added Lady Quest. 'Be very quiet.'

Robin flushed.

'I won't upset him, Lady Quest,' she said.

Dr. Oliver met her outside the door.

'Just a second – and don't excite him, Miss – er – Frayne,' he whispered.

'He isn't mine any more,' thought Robin. 'He is his mother's – he is Dr. Oliver's – he is anybody's but mine – I am only permitted to look at him.'

Aloud she said:

'Will he be all right, doctor?'

'Oh, yes – with time and care. He must be very carefully nursed and treated. Any fresh shock could be very bad for him.'

'He'll have every care here,' said Robin. 'Oh, how thankful I am he did not die.'

'It's a miracle that he escaped,' said the doctor gravely.

A moment later Robin was in the room, which was dim and full of the odour of antiseptics.

'Chris – ' she whispered.

His eyes unclosed. To Robin they looked very dark, very dazed with pain.

'Robin,' he murmured.

'I am here, my darling.'

'Darling, darling Robin – don't leave me.'

'No – no – never. I shall never leave you while you want me, dearest.'

'I am sorry to have been – such an – idiot,' he said with difficulty. 'I shouldn't have let – Henry drive – my car. How is – Henry?'

She dared not tell him that Henry Rushton was dead.

84

'All right – all right, darling. Don't worry about him – only get well and strong yourself, very soon.'

'Of course – I must – we are going to be married next month,' he said slowly, trying to smile at her.

'Of course, Chris,' she murmured.

'Don't – leave me,' he said again. 'I love you so, Robin –'

Then his eyes closed, and he drifted off to sleep again.

Robin rose from her knees and looked up at the doctor. Her eyes were bright with tears.

'He wants me,' she said. 'Ought I to go?'

'He'll sleep now for a bit,' said Dr. Oliver. 'The nurse will be here shortly. When she comes I'll give orders that you're to be sent for whenever he wants you. It won't do to thwart him in anything just now – his temperature will go up at once if he gets excited or distressed.'

CHAPTER IX

THAT evening found no change in Christopher's condition. He slept at intervals under the effect of drugs. When he was not sleeping he was in pain, and had one incessant call – for Robin.

She sat beside him quietly, holding his hand, soothing him. The doctor and the hospital nurse, now in attendance, thought they had never seen anything more beautiful than the look on Robin's small, pale face as she bent over her fiancé.

But downstairs there were bitter feelings against her.

'She seems to have bewitched poor old Chris,' Nancy said, in her blunt way. 'He hasn't asked to see anybody, even Mother – '

Lady Quest, her gentle face unusually hard, flushed and bit her lip.

'Chris is very devoted to his future wife,' she said with an effort.

But Nancy knew that she was envious of the girl who was sitting upstairs with the injured man.

Doria Southway, still in the house, said nothing, but thought much. In her own selfish fashion, she too, was suffering. She was madly in love with Christopher Quest – more than ordinarily jealous of Robin. It enraged her to know that at this very moment Robin was upstairs, at Christopher's side.

She was spitefully pleased when, after dinner that night, Aubrey Mauldron called at the house and asked for Robin. It put Robin in a bad light to have this young man constantly pursuing her. Lady Quest received him coldly; then, remembering he had been at school with her dead nephew, softened a trifle.

'It must have been a shock to you to know that poor Henry was taken from us so suddenly,' she said.

Aubrey, spruce, handsome, over polite as usual, inclined his head.

'I was horribly shocked,' he admitted. 'I heard about the accident at my hotel. I can't believe poor Rushton is dead.'

'He was killed outright – mercifully,' sighed Lady Quest.

'And your son?'

'We have great hopes he will recover.'

'I came to offer my sympathies to Robin,' said Aubrey smoothly. 'But if it is not convenient just now – '

'Not at all,' said Christopher's mother. 'I will send for Robin. She is sitting with my son at the moment, but I may, perhaps, take her place while she talks to you – '

Across the room Doria Southway's blue eyes met Aubrey's. A queer little smile hovered about Doria's mouth. Aubrey flickered his eyebrows, ever so slightly. These two suddenly seemed to read and understand each other. Doria was practically certain that Aubrey was in love with Robin – and trying to take her from Christopher. The thought both intrigued and excited her.

It came as a shock to Robin when Nancy crept into her brother's room and coolly whispered in her ear that Aubrey wished to see her.

She left her fiancé with the greatest reluctance. As she followed Nancy downstairs her cheeks burned and her lips tightened at the thought of Aubrey. How dared he follow her here like this – worry her – when Christopher's life was at stake?

His coming brought back to her mind all the happenings of the last twenty-four hours. Her heart gave a twist of dismay as she remembered her last meeting with Aubrey. She had been forced by Henry Rushton to promise to break her engagement with Chris.

But must she do it now that poor Henry Rushton was dead? She bore him no grudge. She knew that he had acted according to his own light – yet she felt his death to be a release to her – a release from that promise to break that

87

engagement which she held so precious, so dear. Only Aubrey remained to theaten and torture her. But would he prove as ruthless and relentless as Henry had been – now that this terrible accident had taken place?

Hope sprang to Robin's heart. Almost eagerly she approached Aubrey. She must see him, speak to him alone, implore him to put an end to her misery, and go away tomorrow. Surely now that Henry Rushton was no more, he would leave her alone? It was Henry who had been the more imminent danger – who had seen her that fatal night in Aubrey's flat.

Robin tried to greet Aubrey carelessly.

'It is nice of you to come and sympathise,' she forced, giving him her hand. 'But I – I'm afraid I can't stay just now. I – Chris wants me upstairs – '

'I daresay Chris won't mind if his mother takes your place just for a moment,' put in Lady Quest with an acid smile.

Robin flushed scarlet. She felt, rather than saw, the sneer on Doria's beautiful face. She knew they were all jealous of her. But she spoke gently to Christopher's mother.

'Why, of course – please do go to him – he's awake at the moment.'

Aubrey's blue eyes narrowed a trifle. In his astute way he summed up the whole situation and was aware of the strained atmosphere in this household. Robin was by no means wanted here. But he wanted her – how he wanted her! He looked down at her charming face and felt an insane desire to seize her in his arms.

'Perhaps you'd just walk down the garden with me to the gate, Robin,' he said. 'I'll come again tomorrow when you are – er – less occupied.'

'Do,' she forced. 'Yes, I'll walk to the drive with you.'

'She's a terrible flirt. Chris ought to know how she carries on with this man,' Nancy whispered to Doria.

Doria made no answer. But she smiled.

Out in the garden Aubrey and Robin walked down the drive.

'Why did you come?' Robin broke the silence between

them. 'You must have known I wouldn't want to see you tonight with Chris so desperately ill.'

'Of course, I'm very sorry about the accident. It's a nasty business,' said Aubrey glibly. 'And it's awful to think of poor old Rushton – '

Robin shuddered.

'Awful,' she repeated. 'And Chris might have died, too – '

Aubrey paused and took one of her slender wrists.

'Stop a moment, Robin. I want to talk to you,' he said. 'You appear to have forgotten the way our conversation ended this morning.'

She stiffened. Her face, upturned to his, was like a pale mask in the moonlight.

'No – I haven't forgotten. I couldn't possibly forget the vile way you lied to Henry Rushton – the way you allowed him to think unspeakable things about me.'

Aubrey put his tongue in his cheek.

'Are you going to waste your time reproaching me, Robin?'

'No,' she said breathlessly. 'But I'm going to ask you to behave decently, in view of the terrible end Henry met, and of Chris's accident, and go away and put an end to all this.'

His handsome face assumed its obstinate look.

'I won't go away unless you come with me.'

'Oh, am I to argue, to plead with you all over again?' she cried under her breath.

'Don't waste your time,' he said. 'I love you – I mean to have you, Robin.'

'You can't make me break my engagement.'

'I can, and will. Unless you break it I shall tell the Quests myself, that you lived with me in Paris.'

'That's a lie!'

Her voice was passionate and resentful, but he laughed and caught her other wrist.

'Is it? Well, let's make it true. Come with me to Paris – run away with me all over again, little Robin, and this time I swear I'll marry you.'

With loathing in her eyes she tried to drag her hands away.

'I hate you – despise you! Let me go.'

It amused him, soothed his wounded vanity, his thwarted passion, to use sheer physical force on her tonight. He let her writhe and struggle in vain, then flung both arms around her.

'No use – you can't get away, you'll never get away from me, Robin,' he said in a low tense voice.

He pressed his lips hard down on her mouth. It was a long, ruthless kiss that sickened and terrified her. When at last he released her she was white and shaking. Loving Christopher with all her heart and soul it was like death itself to her to be in the arms of this man.

She covered her face with her hands and began to sob in a broken, frightened way.

'Why – why must you torment me? Why can't you go away and leave me alone?'

'Because I want you for myself.'

She raised a face that streamed with scalding tears.

'Have you no decency in you, Aubrey? I love Christopher Quest.'

'You loved me first. You can love me again.'

'Listen,' she said, trying to stifle her sobs. 'The doctor told me this morning that to distress or excite Chris in any way might kill him. If I were to leave him or disillusion him now, it might be his death. Do you want that on your soul?'

Aubrey averted his gaze.

'No, I don't suppose so.'

'Then at least leave me alone until he's better. I ask it for his sake only,' she said.

Aubrey shrugged his shoulders.

'Oh, very well. I'll leave you in peace until Quest is better. But I'll stay near by. I'm not going to lose sight of you, Robin. And as soon as Quest is well, you must break that engagement – or I'll do it for you!'

She wiped her eyes. She was terribly tired of fighting this man– fighting for the happiness of the man she worshipped, as well as her own.

'Very well,' she said. 'Now go, please!'

'Good night, my Robin,' he said.

He turned and walked quickly down the drive, where he was lost to view in the darkness.

Robin wiped her eyes, smoothed her hair, and started to walk back to the house. She had but one desire – to get back to Christopher, to comfort him, help him over his moments of pain, soothe the poor nerves that had been torn to shreds.

But half-way down the drive she paused with a violent start. The tall figure of Doria Southway appeared suddenly from behind some bushes. Robin looked at her with wide, frightened eyes.

'Oh, how you startled me!' she murmured, trying to laugh.

Doria's face was curiously flushed and excited. She came up to Robin and stood looking at her in silence for a moment. Then she said in a cool, modulated voice,

'I won't mince matters; I may as well tell you at once that I was on my way home just now, coming down a side path instead of the main drive, and I overheard your whole conversation with Aubrey Mauldron.'

Robin's heart stopped beating.

'You – heard – ?'

'Yes. I know now exactly what sort of girl you are. And I wonder what my friends the Quests would say,' said Doria in a slow, insulting voice, 'if they knew their son was engaged to be married to *Aubrey Mauldron's mistress*?'

Robin's face went ashen pale. She shook from head to foot. She gasped out,

'It isn't true – it isn't true! Oh, how dare you say such a thing! I am not – I never have been his – his – oh! – ' She broke off and buried her face in her hands. She could not even utter the word.

But Doria felt neither pity nor doubt about it. She gave Robin a cruel look up and down.

'I'm sorry, Robin,' she said, 'but I can't possibly believe anything you say. I overheard the entire conversation. It was conclusive evidence of what you are – what you have been.'

Robin uncovered her face. Her head shot up.

'It isn't true,' she repeated passionately. 'I'm not what you

91

think – what the conversation led you to believe. I'll tell you the whole story if you'll only listen.'

'No, thank you,' said Doria coldly. 'I'd prefer not to hear your sordid tale.'

'It isn't fair of you,' said Robin. 'You must hear me!'

Doria shrugged her shoulders.

'Must I?' she said. 'I'd really rather not. However, if you insist – carry on. It won't alter my belief – my conviction of the kind of girl you are. And from what I can gather, poor Henry Rushton knew too.'

'He made the same mistake you're making,' said Robin, putting her hands up to her cheeks, which were feverishly burning now. 'Since you listened to my conversation with Aubrey, didn't you hear me accuse him of lying to Henry Rushton?'

'Oh, I heard – yes,' drawled Doria. 'But that won't wash. Aubrey kissed you violently, begged you to run away to Paris again – said he'd marry you this time - suggested that he would break your engagement for you if you wouldn't break it yourself.'

'Oh, yes, it all sounds awful,' said poor Robin. 'But I can explain, Doria – I swear I can. Please, please listen – without prejudice.'

Doria twisted her mouth; shrugged her shoulders again.

'Go on – tell me, then,' she said.

Robin prayed dumbly for courage, for strength. She was so tired, so worn with fighting – so sick to the very core about the whole affair. She had been through this very same argument and accusation with Henry Rushton. Now he was dead, and she was facing the battle with a fresh enemy – with Doria Southway. And she realised that Doria was an even more deadly opponent than Henry had been, because she was a woman – and a woman who wanted Christopher Quest for herself.

She blurted out the whole story of how she had gone away with Aubrey Mauldron – his treatment of her – her escape from the Paris flat.

'I swear I've told you the truth,' she finished. 'And I love

Chris with all my heart and soul, have only Chris's happiness at heart.'

As Robin's voice died away Doria stared a moment at the starry sky, thinking, putting two and two together. She was a clever girl – a shrewd one. She knew that Robin had spoken the truth. She believed that story – was certain that Robin was an innocent victim. Aubrey Mauldron was the sort of man no girl could trust. It was all pretty obvious to Doria, woman-of-the-world. But she had not the smallest intention of letting Robin know she believed her.

She wanted Christopher for herself, wanted him to mad-ness. If she could shake his faith in Robin, separate them finally – she might stand an excellent chance of catching Christopher on the rebound.

'Well?' came Robin's voice, in an anguish of anxiety. 'Don't you believe me?'

Very slowly, deliberately came Doria's answer.

'No!'

Robin uttered a cry.

'But you must – you must. Doria, I swear –'

'Please don't prolong this painful scene,' broke in Doria. 'I do not believe you. I am certain you are not what Chris believes you to be. I won't argue or discuss the matter further.'

Robin put a hand up to her head with a gesture of infinite weariness. She had suffered so much, she felt she could not suffer or fight much longer. Everybody seemed to be out to separate her from Christopher. It was useless trying to establish an innocence she could not prove – that Aubrey refused to admit.

'What are you going to do?' asked Robin in a dull voice.

'Tell Lady Quest at once,' said Doria.

'If you do that – if you let Chris know – it might kill him,' said Robin, shutting her eyes. 'He's very ill. Perhaps you forget that. Even Aubrey' – her voice broke on a bitter little laugh – 'even Aubrey is going to wait until Chris is better, before he forces me to break my engagement.'

Doria bit her lower lip. What Robin said was true. Christopher asked incessantly for his fiancée. It might prove fatal to cause an upheaval while he was still in that state of shock and collapse.

'I don't intend to let Chris suffer – at the moment,' she said, after a pause. 'I quite realise that you have wormed your way round him very cleverly, and that he wants you at this crisis. But as soon as the doctors say he is strong enough to bear a fresh shock, I shall ask you to break your engagement, Robin.'

'Doria, you are a friend of Christopher's – but not one of the family, as Henry Rushton was. Do you honestly think you have any right to interfere – to insult me so grossly?'

'Every right,' said Doria, tossing her golden head. 'Before you came I expected to become Chris's wife – but you took him away from me. Once you have gone back to where you belong, I shall probably take your place. Do you see?'

These words were literally flung at Robin – calculated to hurt, to crush what spirit remained in the unhappy girl. They had the desired effect. Robin turned away, her small face a mask of pain. Perhaps Doria spoke the truth, she thought. Perhaps, in days to come, Chris would forget her – and take Doria for his wife.

'Oh, why should I have to bear so much when I am absolutely innocent of wrong!' she cried half aloud. 'Oh, Chris, my darling, how can I leave you –'

'I'll undertake to keep quiet about you until Chris is well,' came Doria's cold, hard voice. 'And when the time comes, I hope you will spare me the unpleasant necessity of telling him about your past, by breaking your engagement and going right away.'

Robin turned round and gave her a long, deep look – an odd look that made Doria feel strangely uncomfortable.

'Yes, I'll do that,' she said in a hollow voice. 'You and Aubrey Mauldron between you leave me no choice. But I hope, for your sake, Doria, that you'll never suffer as you are making me suffer. Good night.'

Doria did not answer. She frowned and turned away from Robin, and walked quickly down the drive to the gates. She could do nothing more tonight. She was going home. But she hated Robina Frayne – Robin, who would now be going back to Christopher's bedside.

'Not for long, though,' she told herself. 'Once he is strong enough, Miss Robin will be turned out of Little Priory. Her day will be over, and mine will begin!'

CHAPTER X

THE nurse in charge of Christopher's case told Lady Quest that Miss Frayne was undoubtedly responsible for Christopher's speedy recovery. The comfort of her presence, the knowledge of her love for him, on that first day, had given him the strength to fight a somewhat fierce battle with his nerves and a high temperature.

After that it was a question of rest, quiet, and time for the broken arm to heal. Within a few days of the accident he was on the high road to recovery. Dr. Oliver said he had a magnificent constitution and that later in his convalescent days it would be only weakness that he would have to conquer.

They were forced to tell him eventually that his cousin had been killed instantaneously. He took the news well, although it upset him badly.

'Poor Henry – poor old chap,' he said to Robin, his boyish face pale and gloomy. 'What a frightful thing! I wish I'd driven the car myself. Henry didn't understand it so well as I did. But the brakes might have gone wrong with me. I suppose it was fate – and couldn't be avoided. Poor Henry!'

At the end of a week he was much better, and the arm was beginning to heal, carefully set and in a splint. Then began the worst time for poor Robin.

Aubrey Mauldron had kept away from her during the last few days, but he was still there – an ever-present menace to her peace of mind. And Doria Southway was an even more imminent danger. She was a near neighbour and constant visitor to Little Priory, and she had just that little and dangerous knowledge of Robin's past. Robin knew that she was

96

waiting – waiting for the hour when she would be forced to end her engagement.

It was a ghastly position. Doria kept her promise to say nothing to the family for the moment. But she treated Robin coldly in public, and with insulting contempt if ever she saw Christopher's fiancée alone. The family were none too charming to Robin. Lady Quest nourished resentment against the girl because Christopher had asked so constantly for her during his illness, and Nancy Quest had never liked or welcomed her as a future relation. Sir James was the only person in the house to treat Robin with kindness, and that was because – man-like – he bore her no resentment, and was not jealous of her. But even he wished secretly that his son and heir had chosen a girl like Doria Southway.

It took all Robin's courage to stand up against things these days. But for Christopher's sake she shouldered her burden and never once complained of her treatment – never allowed him to be depressed or anxious about their future happiness.

It was Christopher's wish that they should get married as soon as he was well enough. And Robin let him make plans – let him talk of their future – agonised by the secret knowledge that those plans could never be carried out – those hopes never materialised. She knew her love and tenderness helped to make him well and strong and that he was making big strides toward recovery because he was so anxious to arrange their marriage.

But her heart was breaking – her very soul torn with the thought that soon – terribly soon now – she would be going away – making some futile excuse to break their engagement.

Doria was waiting to oust her. Aubrey was waiting to follow and persecute her.

There came the day when Doria met Robin alone in the lounge coming in from the garden, and stopped her.

'Robin – Chris is much better,' she said coldly. 'Lady Quest tells me he may be allowed to come down from his room tomorrow.'

'That is so,' said Robin. 'But he's only up in a chair for the first time, and very weak. You can't mean – ?'

'I mean that you must start making your arrangements to break with him and leave here,' said Doria.

'He is very weak yet –'

'I know that,' said Doria. 'But in, say, another five days Chris will be able to bear the – er – unfortunate news. You wish to go quietly and without a fuss. Very well – make your plans to do so. That's all I have to say.'

She moved away, leaving Robin to stand there alone, her mind full of anguished thought.

Christopher had got up today for the first time. Now, after lunch he was resting, and Robin had been out for some fresh air and exercise. She was just going back to him. He hated letting her out of his sight. It was a quarter to four and she knew he would be awake – would want to sit up in his chair again and talk to her.

She was about to move up the wide oak staircase, when a shadow blotted out the sunlight from the open front door. She looked up and saw Aubrey Mauldron standing there. He had walked quietly up the drive. She had not even heard him come. She looked at him dully, without resentment or anger – with nothing but despair in her eyes.

'May I come in, dear Robin?' he greeted her.

'What do you want?' she said.

'You, of course,' he said boldly, advancing to her side. He lifted one of her hands, and raised it to his lips. But at that she recoiled, drew her hand away and shivered.

'Please don't,' she protested.

Aubrey raised his brows, eyed her a second in silence. He was almost shocked at her appearance. He had not seen her since the night of Christopher's accident. She had grown very much thinner and whiter. The strain of Christopher's illness, coupled with the knowledge that she was being driven to leave him, had been eating Robin's very heart – straining all her nerves. She looked utterly worn.

'I say, you don't look very well,' he said rather awkwardly.

She gave a bitter laugh.

'I'm not bursting with health and spirits,' she said. 'Every day I've felt that I'm drawing nearer a – kind of death.'

98

Aubrey's face reddened.

'Do you care for the fellow as much as that, Robin?'

'Yes, as much as that.'

'It isn't very complimentary to me that you should have forgotten me so quickly,' he said.

'Please don't let us start a discussion,' she said, wearily. 'Why have you come?'

'To say it's about time you came away with me,' he said sullenly, staring at her.

'I'm not coming with you. When I go it will be alone. But Chris is still weak, and I – I haven't told him yet –' Her voice faltered.

Aubrey suddenly gripped both her hands and drew her toward him.

'You must tell him soon then,' he said savagely. 'I'm sick of waiting for you. And you are coming with me – you belong to me – you loved me before you loved him.'

Robin was about to answer, to draw away her hands, but another voice interrupted Aubrey – a familiar voice, which sent the blood flaming to her cheeks. She swung round and looked up at the first landing. To her horror she saw Christopher, leaning over the banisters, staring down at her and Aubrey. He was in a blue dressing-down, his arm still in its splint and sling. He had apparently walked out of his bedroom while the nurse was off duty, heard voices downstairs, and had leaned over and seen Robin with Aubrey Mauldron. His eyes looked stricken. He called down to Robin.

'Robin! – tell me it isn't true – tell me that you aren't going away with him!'

Robin tore her hands away from Aubrey's and rushed to the foot of the stairs. She stared up at Chris, much too agitated to think, for a moment, what to say to him. Her main feeling in that instant was fear for him, not for herself. She knew that he was still weak and ill; that a shock like this might undo all the good that had been done.

Christopher started to stumble down the stairs, clinging to the banisters with his uninjured hand.

'Robin – Robin! What does he mean – how can you belong

99

to him? How can you go away with him when you're going to marry me? Robin – '

She gave a stifled cry, then darted forward up the stairs, two at a time, and met Christopher at the bend of the staircase.

'My dear, my dear, don't come down – you aren't nearly strong enough,' she panted. 'Go back – come with me – back to your room, darling.'

He swayed a moment where he stood. She could see that he was shaking from head to foot. He stared down at her with awful eyes.

'No! He said you *belonged to him*. My God! . . . '

'Hush – come back to your room – I – Chris, you aren't strong enough to argue with Aubrey,' Robin began desperately.

Her one clear thought was for him – anxiety lest this should prove too much for him in his weak condition.

'Come back to your room, darling,' she urged. 'I – I'll explain up there.'

'No – here, now – with him present,' said Christopher thickly. 'Let me go – let me get down to him, Robin. Either he's done me an injury or he's insulted you – he must answer to me.'

'Chris,' she said, full of fear for him. He looked livid, dreadful. 'Please, please leave it now. Come back with me to your room.'

For the first time in his life Christopher Quest looked down at Robin with doubt. She flinched as she read what was written in his eyes. But she still fought to save him.

'Come, darling,' she urged. 'Come with me.'

Christopher's gaze sped past her, down to the man who stood in the hall, fingering his lips, looking very awkward and annoyed. A sudden fury of resentment against Aubrey Mauldron flared up within him. How dared that creep say that Robin belonged to him – that she had ever loved him!

He staggered down two steps, past Robin, the blood rushing to his temples.

'Liar!' he said thickly. 'Swine – !'

Only those two words, those two steps. Then the world spun round him. He put out his uninjured hand – grappling with the darkness that came over him.

'Robin!' he called out.

She reached him as he fainted, and had just sufficient strength to support him in her arms, and let him fall gently on to the stairs, so that the broken arm did not suffer. He lay there crumpled up, silent, eyes closed. She bent over him, smoothing the fair hair back from his brow.

'Chris, Chris – Chris –'

She knew that the fool's paradise in which they had lived was finished. Chris would never believe in her or want her again.

Aubrey Mauldron came quickly up the stairs. When he had seen Christopher stagger and fall, he had wished for a fleeting moment that he had left Robin and her fiancé alone. He touched the kneeling girl on the shoulder.

'Robin,' he said in a low voice. 'I say – I'm sorry –'

'Oh, go – go away!' she said, with passionate emphasis. 'You've done enough harm.'

'Robin, you'd far better come away with me –' he began.

She had no time to answer. At that moment Nancy Quest and Doria Southway appeared, laughing and talking. Then as they simultaneously caught sight of the huddled group on the bend of the staircase, they both stood still and stared.

Nancy caught sight of her brother's fair head, cradled on Robin's arm. She gave a cry and rushed toward him.

'Chris! It's Chris!'

'Chris!' echoed Doria. She followed Nancy, her face flushing with excitement and some consternation.

'What's happened? What's happened?' Nancy gasped in a hysterical voice. 'Oh, look at him – he looks as though he were dead –'

Robin looked at Christopher's young sister.

'No, no, Nancy – he isn't dead – he has fainted – he insisted on coming down the stairs –' she stammered. 'Send for the nurse – we must get him up to his room.'

Nancy swung round on Aubrey Mauldron, looked at him with suspicion and resentment.

'What are you doing here?' she asked rudely.

He flushed and began to walk down the stairs. As he passed Doria, she gave him a long, deep look of inquiry. He met it – shrugged his shoulders.

'I'm sorry,' he murmured. 'Christopher overheard a conversation between Robin and myself – er – he didn't like. I'd better go, I suppose.'

'Ah!' said Doria, under her breath.

Fierce exultation gripped her. She could guess exactly what had happened. Christopher had accidentally come upon a love scene between Mauldron and Robin. Oh, well, it was bound to happen sooner or later! Why not now? It was high time Robin Frayne left this house for ever.

Without a trace of pity she walked to Robin's side.

'Leave Chris alone,' she said in a tone of command. 'His nurse – his sister – or I – will see to him.'

Robin's head shot up.

'How dare you – ' she began.

'It's no good trying to brazen it out,' interrupted Doria cruelly. 'I can see what has happened. Chris has found out about you at last. You had better pack up your things and follow Aubrey Mauldron.'

Nancy stared at her friend.

'Doria – what are you saying?' she gasped.

'You'll know soon,' said Doria. 'I'll explain to you all later. We'd better get Chris to bed, now.'

Robin grew calm. She knew it was no use fighting any longer – that the odds were against her. It was best to surrender quietly.

Doria knew. Doria would tell the family now. And Christopher knew, too. Not much – but enough to shake his faith in her and perhaps destroy his love. With aching eyes she looked down at his white face. He was in a dead faint – and at peace. But once he recovered consciousness, he would suffer horribly. And she could do nothing to prevent it. She rose from her knees. Nancy, only too pleased to see her humiliated and hurt, thrust her roughly away and supported her brother's head on her arm now.

The hospital nurse, flustered and agitated, came hurrying down the stairs to her patient.

Robin was pushed to one side. Doria, Nancy, and the nurse, between them, lifted the unconscious man and carried him up to his room. Sir James and Lady Quest were in the garden, happily ignorant of the drama taking place in the house.

Robin found herself quite alone. She had been shut out – for good. She knew exactly what would happen. If she tried to seek Christopher she would be grossly insulted and turned away.

Quite probably, when he first came to his senses, he would ask for her – demand to see her – to hear her explanation of everything. She asked herself, dully, what she should do – stay and explain and beg him to believe in her innocence – or go away without seeing him again.

Supposing she told him what had happened and asked him to believe in her – supposing he said he would believe, despite all that Aubrey Mauldron had to say or suggest – supposing out of his great love for her, he begged her to remain here and marry him just the same? Could she stay and become his wife, knowing there must be some doubt at the back of his mind – that at times he would be suspicious and distrustful? And all his people would be against the marriage – hate her, look upon her as an adventuress.

Robin covered her face with her hands. She was tortured beyond endurance by her thoughts – her imagination. And she knew when she had thought everything over and considered every possibility, that she could not stay and marry Christopher, even if he wanted her to do so. She could never bear the moments of doubt and disbelief. And Aubrey Mauldron was merciless; would never clear her name.

There was but one thing left to her to do – to go away without seeing Christopher again.

She let her arms drop to her sides limply. She moved slowly up the stairs to her own room.

Doria Southway met her a quarter of an hour later, coming out of that room, dressed for travelling and carrying a suitcase. Doria gave her a quick, sullen look.

'So you are going!' she said. 'Very wise.'

'Yes, I am going,' said Robin. 'Would you be kind enough to ask the chauffeur to drive me to the station. I'll pick up a train for town when I can.'

'Very well,' said Doria.

'I am going because I think it best – for Chris,' added Robin, looking down at the ground, 'not because I am guilty of what you think.'

There was something so quiet, so simple about Robina Frayne in this moment, that even Doria felt a tinge of shame as she looked at her.

'I don't know what to think,' she muttered, 'but I'm sure it's best for you to go.'

'Yes,' said Robin. 'Is Chris better?'

'He is beginning to come round,' said Doria in a grudging voice. 'The nurse says he is all right. He fainted from weakness more than anything.'

'Thank God!' said Robin, with a deep sigh.

She took a letter from her pocket.

'May I trust you to give this to him from me?' she added.

'Yes, I'll give it to him.'

'And my trunk – if you would have it sent to the luggage office at Victoria, I'll fetch it there,' added Robin.

'I don't live in this house,' muttered Doria. 'But I'll give Lady Quest your message. I'm just going into the garden to tell them about things.'

Robin bit her lower lip. Once she had loved Christopher's mother – longed for Lady Quest to love her. But now all that was finished – and Lady Quest would think of her with horror and contempt – think the worst.

She drove away from Little Priory feeling like one in a nightmare. She had no idea where she was going or what she meant to do. She could think of nothing but Christopher. But she remained calm and composed until she found herself alone in a second class carriage of the train to Victoria. Then she broke down and buried her face in her hands and sobbed like one whose heart is broken.

*　　*　　*

Robin left chaos at Little Priory.

When Christopher recovered consciousness he demanded, as she had expected he would do, to see her. The nurse told him that Robin was 'out', and that he must lie quiet. She was not too pleased with her patient. He was still much too white and weak. Obviously he had had some shock. Miss Nancy had intimated at some 'disturbance' between him and his fiancée, and Miss Frayne had left the house. But the news must be broken to the patient gently.

Christopher, weak though he was, however, had strength enough to insist upon his orders being obeyed.

'I wish to see Miss Frayne – at once!' he told the nurse.

The good woman, flurried and worried, went downstairs to where the family were gathered in the drawing-room. Doria was still with them, nursing secret satisfaction to herself, whilst pretending grief on their behalf. Sir James and Lady Quest had been told about Robin and Aubrey Mauldron. Doria had repeated the conversation she had overheard in the garden. She had said enough to convince the family that Robin was unworthy of Christopher's love.

Sir James looked deeply troubled and shocked. Lady Quest was weeping. Nancy marched up and down the room, tossing her untidy mane of hair.

'I don't see why we need waste any tears. She was deceitful. It was a good thing we found out – an escape for poor Chris!' she was saying.

The nurse interrupted by saying that Mr. Quest insisted on seeing Miss Frayne.

The members of the family exchanged glances. Finally, Lady Quest said, handkerchief pressed to her red-rimmed eyes, '

'Doria dear, you know more than any of us – and you are an old friend of dear Chris's. Possibly he would resent your explanation of that girl's absence less than ours. You have a

105

letter from her for him, too, haven't you?'

'Yes,' said Doria, nodding her golden head. 'Shall I go up to him?'

'Do, my dear,' said Lady Quest mournfully.

Doria's heart leaped when she entered Christopher's room and approached his bed. This was her hour. She meant to make the best of it.

Christopher, moving restlessly on his pillows, stared at the tall, golden-haired girl.

'Doria!' he said in surprise.

'Yes, Chris,' she said. 'I've come to talk to you.'

'It is kind of you, but I want Robin,' he said feverishly. 'I particularly want to see her. You don't understand what happened – '

'Yes, my dear, I do,' Doria broke in gently, drawing a chair up to his bedside. 'I know everything. I knew before you did.'

He stared up at her, his eyes burning.

'About what?'

'About that time and Aubrey Mauldron.'

Christopher moistened his dry lips with his tongue.

'Doria, I can't discuss it with you. You don't know what I feel. That fellow – he insulted Robin – he suggested unspeakable things – I tried to get to him, but I'm so damnably weak – I fainted. I must see Robin.'

'My dear, Robin isn't here.'

Christopher's heart missed a beat.

'What do you mean?' he gasped.

'She's gone, Chris – left Little Priory for good.'

He stared at the girl in amazement.

'Gone!' he broke out. 'Who let her go? Who let her go – without seeing me first?'

'She went of her own accord,' said Doria. 'And Aubrey Mauldron – '

'Has gone with her?'

'I don't know. But he went by the same train, anyhow.'

Christopher's face twisted. Drops of moisture rolled from his forehead.

'Doria, what does all this mean?'

She told him. She said she had known for some time that Aubrey Mauldron was a former lover of Robin's. She repeated the conversation she had overheard between Robin and Aubrey in the garden – repeated it so cleverly that Robin was thoroughly incriminated. In so many words, she definitely stated that Robin had lived with Aubrey in Paris, and that Henry Rushton had known it – had been introduced to Robin as Aubrey's wife in Paris; that that was why Henry had always treated Robin coldly, without any cordiality.

Christopher listened to all this in silence. Every word cut him like a knife.

'Doria,' he said. 'Do you swear you have told me the truth?'

'I swear it, Chris!'

'And she has gone – left no message for me?'

Doria gave him the letter Robin had written.

Weakly Christopher tore open the envelope and read the note Robin had left for him.

'Chris, my darling, my beloved, I know things will look black against me and that they will lead you to believe I am guilty. I was in Paris with Aubrey Mauldron, but only for a few hours. I did not live with him. But he has let everybody believe that I did, and I cannot prove that I did not. I am going away because I can never, never marry you with such a shadow between us. But I will always, always love and adore you. Forgive me for not telling you before about Aubrey. I was too frightened. I love you so. Goodbye, Chris,

'ROBIN.'

He read the letter twice. When at length he raised his head some of the pain had gone from his eyes. To him every word she had written rang with sincerity. 'I was too frightened – I love you so.' The words haunted him. Too frightened – of losing him, of losing his love – poor child, poor little Robin!

'Doria,' he said. 'Robin says she is innocent.'

'But you can't possibly believe that!'

'I do believe it,' said Christopher quietly, folding the note

107

and putting it under his pillow. 'And now my one wish is to get strong enough to follow and find Robin and bring her back again.'

Doria rose. She was trembling with anger.

'You must be mad, Chris.'

'Perhaps,' he said, with a short laugh. 'Apparently you don't know the meaning of love – of real love such as mine is for Robin – hers for me – '

'And supposing you find her – with the other man?'

Christopher's face flushed with anger, then grew deadly white. He looked with steady eyes up at the face of Doria Southway.

'Then I shall come back alone,' he said. 'But I'm convinced I shall not find that. Have you Robin's address?'

'No,' said Doria. 'She left no address.'

'That'll make things harder. But I'll find her,' said Christopher. 'You can tell Mother and the others what I say. Now please leave me, Doria. I feel tired – '

She walked out of the room, infuriated.

But Christopher turned his face to the pillow and felt suddenly at peace.

CHAPTER XI

ROBIN stepped out of the train at Victoria. She walked mechanically down the platform, her suitcase in her hand. Her eyes were red-rimmed with weeping. She had cried herself sick and blind all the way up from Horsham. Nobody looked at her. It was the busy hour at Victoria, and she was only one of a teeming crowd; city men rushing to catch their home-bound trains.

She stood a moment by the bookstall and stared blindly at the rows of paperbacks in their attractive wrappers. She saw the title of one: *Goodbye to All That*. She had read it down at Little Priory. Lady Quest had had it from the library. It was a war book. She felt as though she had just been through a dreadful, terrible war . . . a personal Hell. She had come out of it horribly scarred. And it was all so unfair and so unnecessary. She had not committed a sin – she had only been stupidly indiscreet and over-trusting when she had run away to Paris and Aubrey. But she was suffering as badly as though she had committed a crime.

She could hardly believe that she was never going to see Christopher again. *Goodbye to All That!* . . . to all her hopes of happiness. Poor Chris! And he'd be so wretched and unhappy, too. She paid herself the compliment of believing that he'd regret her.

What was she going to do now? It was almost like history repeating itself. She felt as she had felt that night in Paris when she had run away from Aubrey's flat. Derelict . . . at the end of all things. But it hadn't been the end then. She had found a haven with kind Grace Williamson. It had meant the beginning of a lot of happiness. It seemed unutterably sad that such happiness had been taken from her and Christopher – unjustly.

While she stood there, hesitating, she saw a man in grey, carrying a suitcase, swing down the platform toward her. The blood rushed to her face as she recognised Aubrey Mauldron. As he reached her side she stepped back a pace.

'You – you followed me, Aubrey?'

'Of course. I watched you leave Little Priory and caught the same train, only we travelled in different carriages,' said Aubrey. 'My dear little girl, you met with all this trouble through – er – through me. Did you think I'd let you face the world alone?'

Robin's eyes gleamed with anger.

'You had no right to follow me. You've done me enough wrong,' she said. 'Leave me alone, or you'll drive me mad!'

'Now, listen, Robin,' he said. 'You're up here in London with no money, I'm certain, and nowhere to go. Quest has finished with you. You can't marry him now, can you?'

'No.'

'Well, then, be sensible and marry me,' he said. 'I've got plenty of money and you used to care for me once. You'll care for me again. Come, Robin, let me take you to an hotel and leave you there and tomorrow we'll get married by special licence.'

She shuddered and looked at him with eyes of loathing.

'No, never. Go away. Leave me alone.'

'Come along,' he said, quietly taking her arm. 'Don't waste time fighting me. One day you'll have to come to me. You might as well save a lot of trouble and come now.'

She shivered and turned from him.

'I'd starve in the gutter before I'd come to you for help.'

'You have no money – nowhere to go,' he said. 'Why be such a little fool? Marry me and you'll have everything money can buy. I'll be good to you, Robin. I swear it.'

'Good to me?' She laughed bitterly. 'I don't want your goodness. And I prefer any privation or hardship to luxury at such a price. It makes me sick even to imagine myself in your arms.'

'Come,' he insisted. 'You must, Robin. You're done with Quest. Put it all out of your mind and come with me.'

She shrank away from him.

'Oh, leave me alone,' she implored.

'I shall never leave you alone,' he said. 'Never until you marry me.'

Robin pressed a hand to her forehead. The pain in her temples was so intense she felt sick, blind with it. This persistent persecution from Aubrey was more than she could bear. She felt that she had neither the physical nor the mental strength to endure it.

'But I shall never give way to him,' she told herself. 'Never. He will never win.'

'Come, Robin,' he repeated. 'It's time we left the platform. People are staring.'

She allowed him to take her outside the station. Taxi-cabs rolled up and away. Porters shouted; vans rattled; people rushed hither and thither. The noise made the pain in her head worse. Aubrey looked down at her white little face.

'Look here, Robin,' he said, in a tone of contrition. 'Don't look like that. It makes me feel such a brute, and –'

'What does that matter?' she broke in. 'You are a brute, but feeling it doesn't help you to do the right thing.'

'I want to do the right thing – to marry you.'

'That isn't right. That's all wrong. I love Christopher Quest, and I hate you.'

He sighed.

'How obstinate you can be! Oh, well, I'm going to be patient. I know you'll come to me in the end.'

'If you worry me much longer you'll drive me insane,' she said, with an hysterical laugh. 'Then you can have me – a mad woman – if you like. I shouldn't care!'

'Rubbish. You want a stiff brandy and soda and a good night's rest, my dear girl,' he said calmly.

'What a cruel beast you are!' she said.

'Taxi!' called Aubrey.

Robin's heart began to race. She was genuinely afraid of Aubrey now. She was not going to be bullied into accompanying him to an hotel. She would not go with him.

The taxi rolled up. Aubrey took her arm.

'Jump in, my dear,' he said.

'No,' said Robin in a smothered voice. 'You have no right— no right at all – I want to go my own way – oh, for pity's sake – '

Her voice was drowned in the rattle of a passing trolley. She felt dizzy, weak with protesting and arguing. Aubrey's strong arm literally pushed her into the taxi. She found herself in it, driving out of Victoria Station toward the West End.

Aubrey gave a grim smile and touched her knee.

'No use fighting me, Robin,' he said. 'You've just got to give in.'

She shrank as far from him as she could get in her corner of the taxi, one hand pressed to her aching forehead. If she had felt well, strong physically, she could have fought him so much better. But all she had been through, and lack of food, had made her wretchedly weak and incapable of asserting her will power.

'Oh, let me be,' she whispered. 'Can't you see that I don't want to marry you? I won't! I won't!'

'Yes, you will,' he said coolly.

She stared at him with eyes that seemed blurred.

'When this taxi stops, I shall get out and leave you,' she said, in a hoarse, little voice. 'I'm going my own way – you shan't stop me, you devil!'

'Come, come, Robin,' he laughed. 'Don't lose your temper. Now, honestly, my dear child, where can you go, and what can you do? You've no money beyond a pound or two in your bag, and no job. Your own family won't have you, and Lady Quest won't give you a reference after what has happened. You'll be better off in my care, I assure you.'

Robin tried to speak, to argue, but no words came. The buzzing pain in her head was growing worse. She felt desperately ill and desperately frightened.

She heard Aubrey's voice from far, far off.

'What's the matter, Robin? Feeling ill?'

He was really anxious now. She looked ghastly white and

her eyelids were closing. He took the seat beside her and put an arm around her shoulders.

'Robin! I say – are you going to faint?'

She was dimly conscious of his arm about her – his handsome face bending over her. She made a feeble effort to speak, to protest. Then she lost consciousness.

Aubrey felt the slim little body sag. Her head fell forward on his breast. He realised that she had fainted. It had all been too much for her. And it was no ordinary faint. She was very ill, obviously. Perhaps her brain had been affected by the shock of recent events.

Aubrey's heart beat quickly and he bit his lip, as he stared down at her. The fact that she was helpless now, unable to defend herself, aroused no chivalry in him. He only realised with a thrill of excitement that she was absolutely in his power.

By the time the taxi had reached a certain hotel in Piccadilly, he had formed a clever plan.

He assumed an expression of grave anxiety as the smart commissionaire opened the taxi door.

'My wife is ill – has fainted,' he said briefly. 'Help me carry her into the hotel. We've come from Victoria and were intending to stay in town a few days.'

The man was all respectful concern. Robin was very light – much too thin and light. She was soon carried out of the taxi, through the lounge, past a crowd of curious people, into the passenger lift.

Aubrey coolly booked an expensive suite of rooms, and signed the register 'Mr. and Mrs. Aubrey Mauldron'. A few minutes later he was standing in the luxurious sitting-room of his suite, giving instructions to the maid for whom he had rung.

'My wife is delicate, and subject to bad fainting fits. Will you see if you can bring her round,' he said. 'I have asked the porter to send for a doctor.'

The maid hurried into the adjoining room. Robin had been laid on the big bed. She looked like a child, her dark head sunk in the pillows, her eyes still shut.

Aubrey walked into the room and watched the maid deftly remove Robin's coat and bathe her head with eau-de-Cologne.

'Madame looks bad, sir,' she said. 'Don't you think some brandy –'

'Yes. There's a flask in my suitcase. I'll fetch it,' said Aubrey.

He behaved like an anxious, dutiful husband. The maid thought him most handsome and most charming. Madame was fortunate to be married to such a pleasant gentleman.

The brandy had no effect upon Robin. She stirred, choked, moaned a little, then lay still again. She was certainly in no light faint.

Aubrey began to grow nervous. He was relieved when the doctor arrived. By that time the maid had undressed Robin and got her into bed. Aubrey had half unpacked his things in his own bedroom, which led out of Robin's.

Aubrey lied smoothly to the doctor.

His wife was not at all strong – had found the train journey trying – was easily overcome by heat – had been dazed, wandering in her mind for some days – he was horribly worried, etc., etc.

The doctor gave him a few encouraging words and made an examination of Robin. He did not for an instant doubt that she was Mrs. Mauldron. In the taxi, Aubrey had slid a platinum wedding ring on Robin's finger. He was a man of experience and adventure, and that ring travelled with him.

The verdict of the physician was 'a bad nervous breakdown' due to great mental strain or shock. Mrs. Mauldron would probably recover consciousness soon. She must have the utmost care and quiet and would need a hospital nurse.

Aubrey – the anxious husband – sat by Robin's bedside, watching, waiting for her to awake. He must be there, he reflected, to tell Robin what he had done. It seemed to him that under the awkward circumstances she would have no choice but to give in to him – Fate had literally pushed her into his arms.

It was late that night when Robin opened her eyes, and came out of that long swoon. Perplexedly, she stared round the big bedroom – then at two figures – one hatefully familiar – the other a strange hospital nurse in a spotless white apron and cap.

She lifted a hand to her head. She felt remarkably weak and feeble, and when she spoke it was in the veriest whisper.

'Aubrey – '

She spoke the name of the man because she knew him – because she was terrified and dazed and did not know where she was or what had happened.

Aubrey at once left the nurse's side and came to her, knelt down and took her hands, his heart racing.

'Robin – oh, my darling – you are awake at last!' he said loudly, for the nurse's benefit. Then he whispered rapidly against her ear: 'Listen, Robin – don't make a fuss – you fainted in the taxi – I brought you here, up to this suite, as my wife – the doctor has seen you – everybody thinks you are Mrs. Mauldron – take my advice and don't undeceive them and cause a fuss and scandal, otherwise I'll make sure Christopher hears about you staying here with me – '

Weak, ill though she felt, Robin understood quite clearly all that he said. She grew more frightened, felt more helpless than ever. But she said nothing. What could she do? He had taken full advantage of her fainting fit. She was here in this hotel as his wife – she saw the strange wedding ring on her finger. He had won – at least for the time being – until she was well enough to get away from him. Despair settled over her.

'You'll soon be all right, darling,' he said, stroking her hair – still for the benefit of the nurse – and against her ear, on pretence of kissing her cheek, 'Don't worry, Robin. Just lie quiet and get better. I swear I'll marry you as soon as you'll agree to it, and I won't touch a hair of your head until you are really my wife.'

She shuddered.

'Chris,' she inwardly cried. 'Chris – what would you say if

you knew? Oh, it isn't my fault – I tried so hard to fight –'

She was too ill and tired to fight any more.

*   *   *

So long as Robin was really ill, Aubrey was comparatively kind and sincerely anxious on her behalf. But when a week of this farce had passed, and Robin was growing stronger and declaring her intention of getting up and sending the nurse away, he showed himself the kind of man he really was.

He was quite aware that this position distressed and tortured the girl – that she hated being confined to the hotel bedroom as Mrs. Aubrey Mauldron. But it amused him considerably, and he felt confident that Robin would have no alternative now but to marry him.

Robin said little, but all the time she lay there in the big, luxurious bed, surrounded by all the comforts money could buy, she was silently awaiting the hour when she could get up and leave Aubrey for ever.

'I was ill and weak when I left Little Priory,' she told herself. 'But I shan't faint or give in again – next time I make up my mind to escape Aubrey, I shall succeed.'

Her one desire now was to get well. She obeyed the doctor who attended her; ate the food given to her; tried to remain quiet. Whenever she remembered Christopher her pain was almost unendurable. She wondered how he had taken the news of her departure – what he thought of her. She prayed he did not think too badly. She loved him so. She would never, never forget the beauty, the sweetness of their love. As for really becoming the wife of Aubrey Mauldron – the mere thought sickened her.

Whenever Aubrey entered her bedroom her small face grew rigid – her eyes dark with hatred. He knew just how she felt about him. So now, when she was stronger, he took pleasure in tormenting her, knowing she dared not repulse him.

One afternoon he came and sat on the edge of her bed and put his arms round her in front of the nurse, who thought Robin a fortunate girl to possess so delightful a husband. Th

116

bedroom was full of flowers – great dewy roses, huge masses of lilac, hot-house carnations – all from Aubrey. On the table beside her stood a bowl of fruit – an expensive box of French chocolates – a pile of the latest illustrated magazines – some new novels. What more could a husband buy for his wife? The nurse was rather nettled with Robin for being so cool, so seemingly ungrateful to her husband.

Aubrey, with a charming smile on his handsome face, played with Robin's hands, quite aware that she shivered from the contact with him.

'You're much better, aren't you, darling?' he murmured. 'Tomorrow nurse thinks you'll be able to get up, and the day after, if it keeps fine, you shall come out for a drive.'

Robin's eyes narrowed. She said nothing, but silently she decided that if she was strong enough to go out for a drive she would be strong enough to steal out unnoticed, take a taxi, and escape from this man altogether.

'How adorable you look in your new nightie, Robin,' said Aubrey.

Her heart beat with anger. How she hated him – hated the presents he had showered on her. Never could she forgive him for this dastardly trick. He had fetched her trunk from Victoria, and then ordered piles of expensive clothes from West End shops. Silk underwear; glamorous nighties; a heavy satin dressing-gown; a lovely gold and blue Chinese bed-jacket, heavily embroidered. Her face was white and thin in its frame of dark hair, but she looked lovely enough to fascinate any man. Aubrey's pulses missed a beat as he looked down at her. Everybody believed her to be his wife – his wife –

'You beautiful thing!' he suddenly said, bending over her. She flushed scarlet.

'Please!' she protested under her breath. 'Please go out of my room, Aubrey.'

But he lost his head. Suddenly he caught her close to him and crushed her lips in a kiss.

The nurse discreetly tip-toed out of the room.

For a moment, in tense silence, Robin fought with Aubrey. Her heart beat with suffocating speed. She burned with anger

117

and shame. Brute, beast, to take such advantage of the position in which he had placed her against her knowledge and will! She struggled in his arms.

'Let me go! Aubrey – you beast!'

He buried his face against her soft throat.

'My wife,' he said with a mocking smile. 'Mine.'

It was more than Robin could bear.

'Nurse! Nurse!' she called out.

The good woman came hurrying in. Perforce Aubrey sprang up from the bed and walked to the window, his face crimson. Robin held out a trembling hand to the nurse.

'I – feel – faint,' she gasped. 'I – I'm afraid I scared – my husband.'

Aubrey's lips curled in an ugly smile.

She had got the better of him this time. Well, she would see. He would win her in the end. He walked out of the room, jammed a hat fiercely on his head, and marched out of the hotel.

The nurse, thinking 'Mrs. Mauldron' had been over-excited, tucked her up, drew the curtains, and bade her sleep until tea-time.

Robin lay still on her pillows, her eyes shut.

'Oh, Chris, Chris, I want you so,' she inwardly groaned.

She was growing terrified of Aubrey. Tomorrow she must get away – somehow.

That next morning Aubrey had to go out on business. He announced his intention of returning at midday to take Robin for a drive. It was a brilliant summer's morning, and the doctor said the fresh air would do her good – bring some colour to her cheeks.

Robin resorted to cunning in her desperate desire to escape Aubrey.

'I'd like to go out alone with my – my husband,' she murmured to the nurse, her thin face flushing. 'You take the rest of the morning off, nurse, and when Mr. Mauldron comes back he'll find me alone, waiting for him.'

The nurse thought that a pretty idea. She dressed her patient, wrapped her in a fur coat, and left her.

As soon as the woman had gone, Robin darted to the wardrobe – pulled out her own old shabby suit and re-dressed herself. With loathing and contempt she flung Aubrey's presents away from her. She packed the suitcase and prepared to run away. She felt weak and her hands trembled as she moved. But she was much better – well enough to get away, she told herself. Get away she must.

Her heart raced with excitement as she stole out of the corridor and down in the lift. She was terrified that Aubrey might meet her. But the coast was clear. In another moment she was in a taxi, with her own modest belongings and a few pounds in her bag, bound for a cheap, private hotel in Bayswater.

It must have been exactly five minutes later that another taxi rolled up to the hotel Robin had just left, and a tall, thin, good-looking young man, with grey eyes and fair hair, and his left arm in a sling, got out and walked into the vestibule.

It was Lieut.-Commander Christopher Quest.

Christopher, too, had escaped from doctors and nurses and deliberately come up to London to find the girl he had worshipped and in whom he still believed.

He was by no means strong. His face looked pale and weary and he had lost all his old buoyancy and strength. But he walked firmly to the desk to book his room. It was by a strange coincidence that he had chosen this very hotel. But it was one of the most comfortable in town, and he had been here before. He had no notion where Robin was, but he knew she was in London; that her luggage had been sent from Little Priory to Victoria. He was determined to engage the services of the best detective in London to trace her, if need be. He loved her. He wanted her. The chagrin and anger of the family did not matter to him. Nothing mattered – except Robin.

Signing the register, he ran his gaze idly down the list of names. And suddenly his thin face flushed scarlet and his heart gave a great bound. He had seen the entry – Mr. and Mrs. Aubrey Mauldron.

As Christopher stared blindly at that damning piece of

evidence, his haggard young face grew whiter and for a moment he felt, not merely misery, but hot rage in his heart. Rage against Aubrey Mauldron for taking the woman he had loved and wanted for his wife – anger against Robin for being false to all her promises – all her vows. He had trusted her absolutely. He felt the most passionate resentment against her for breaking his faith, breaking his heart.

So everything they had insinuated at home had had foundation. Everything Doria had said about Robin was true. She had just played with him – she had left him for a former lover.

The anger died down in Christopher. It was replaced by a strange disbelief – a strange feeling that it was not the Robin he had loved and trusted who had let him down like this. He began to question the reception-clerk in a low, terse voice.

'I see some friends of mine – Mr. and Mrs. Mauldron – are here. When did they come?'

'Eight or nine days ago.'

'Do you know – Mrs. Mauldron well by sight? Could you – describe her to me?'

The reception-clerk glanced curiously at Christopher's white, unhappy face.

'Yes,' she said. 'She came to the hotel in rather a dramatic fashion. She was carried in from a taxi unconscious.'

Christopher's heart leaped. His eyes dilated with sudden excitement.

'Unconscious? Why? What was the matter?'

'She was very ill – had fainted in the taxi, I was told. She was carried up to her room by her husband and a porter. Such a sweet, pretty little thing – I saw her with her dark head, leaning on her husband's shoulder – dark, wavy hair.'

'Yes, yes,' said Christopher, his lips dry, his heart racing. 'That's the Mrs. Mauldron I know. But when did this happen?'

The clerk told him the exact date and time. Christopher pieced the bits of information together. He deduced that Robin must have come up from Horsham almost immediately after he had discovered her with Aubrey that day and fainted on the stairs. From the time it appeared she must have come

120

straight to the hotel from Victoria. How, then, could she be married to Mauldron – unless she had been married to him before? But that was incredible, impossible.

Strange thoughts chased through Christopher's brain. Robin – for Robin it must be from the clerk's description – had been taken up to the suite booked by Aubrey, insensible, and had been in bed ever since. She was up there now, ill. Perhaps she had been drugged – perhaps this had all been done against her will!

'What is the number of the Mauldrons' suite?' he asked the clerk feverishly. 'I'd like to go up – to see Mrs. Mauldron.'

'One moment,' said the girl. 'I'll ring up and ask if you can. What name shall I say?'

'Mr. Quest.'

Another few moments and Robin's absence from her bedroom and the hotel was discovered. The reception-clerk shrugged her shoulders.

'I don't know where she is, I'm sure,' she said, in answer to Christopher's anxious inquiries. 'I thought she was still in bed. Mr. Mauldron is out. So is the hospital nurse in attendance.'

Christopher's brain seethed. Every moment he grew more and more certain that there was something odd about this – that Robin had been brought here and detained against her will. Yes, he was certain of it. And if she had run away today, he would find her.

He rushed through the lounge to the hall-porter – shot a few rapid questions at him. The man answered with intelligence. Yes, he had seen a lady he thought to be Mrs. Mauldron come out this morning, carrying a suitcase. He had called a taxi for her.

'Well – did you hear her give the driver an address?' demanded Christopher.

'I did, sir, but I forget – '

'Try to remember,' interrupted Christopher, his cheeks feverishly flushed. He slid a note into the man's hand.

The porter's eyes beamed. He broke into a smile and scratched his head.

'I think the lady said 24, or 34, Coherne Street, S.W. Wait a bit, sir – or was it an 'otel – yes, it was – the Coherne Hotel, Bayswater.'

Christopher's pulses thrilled. Anger, misery, all sensations had died within him, save the feeling that he was on the track of a great discovery – that at the Coherne Hotel, wherever that was, he would find Robin and make her explain to him.

At that precise moment, while he stood on the steps of the hotel talking to the hall-porter, a beautiful car, with a gleaming silver bonnet, roared up to the entrance. Christopher glanced at it idly at first. Then his face grew set, and he stiffened in every limb. Out of that car stepped a slim, dark man, with a soft hat at a jaunty angle on his head, and a cigarette between his lips – Aubrey Mauldron.

Christopher was feeling none too strong for an encounter of this kind, but he plunged into it in his boyish, hot-headed way. He regarded Mauldron with suspicion and dislike. He did not mean to miss this opportunity of facing him.

Aubrey was both amazed and dismayed to see Christopher Quest at the hotel, but he greeted him with insolent nonchalance.

'Hullo, Quest. What are you doing up in town?'

Christopher walked up to him and met his gaze levelly.

'I've come up to find Robin,' he said.

Aubrey put his tongue in his cheek.

'Well?' he drawled. 'She's my wife.'

'I'm not sure of that,' said Christopher tersely. 'I'm not at all sure that isn't a damnable lie. At any rate, I have to prove it yet.'

'My dear fellow – Robin is very ill and up in her bedroom –' began Aubrey.

'That is where you are wrong,' broke in Christopher, with a feeling of satisfaction. 'Robin is not in the hotel.'

Aubrey's face changed colour.

'Then where is she?'

'At an hotel in Bayswater. I know the address. It is all very odd. Why should your wife – if she is your wife – take advantage of your absence to leave the hotel with her

122

luggage? It looks to me as though she was forced here against her will.'

Aubrey bit his lip. He felt suddenly furious that Robin had escaped from him.

'Oh, damn it all,' he said violently. 'I'm getting sick of Robin – and of you!'

Christopher's hand shot out and gripped his arm.

'Not so fast, Mauldron. You're coming with me.'

'Oh, am I?' sneered Aubrey. 'And where?'

'To Robin. You are going to face her in front of me and explain all this,' said Christopher through clenched teeth. 'There is too much mystery about it all. I don't believe Robin is married to you, and I don't believe she cares an ounce for you. You've got some hold over her, no doubt, which made her leave home and me, but you're going to explain it all, or – by heaven! – I'll make you pay!'

Aubrey opened his lips as though to speak, then shut them again. He shot Christopher a look of vicious hatred. But he was a physical coward as well as a moral blackguard, and he saw that Christopher would keep his word. He had only one free arm, but he could probably use that one fist to advantage – and would. Aubrey sized up his man pretty well.

He imagined he had won Robin; had thought himself on the point of getting her. But Robin had gone, and Quest had found her. Well, what use to pursue her any longer? He was genuinely sick of it all. He had money, looks, position – why throw himself away on a girl who hated him and whined all day for another man? He had been a fool – a stubborn fool – ever to set his heart on getting Robin.

'Well?' rapped out Christopher. 'What have you to say?'

'Nothing much,' said Aubrey, with a short laugh, 'except that you've won, Quest, and I'm too sick of the whole business to worry about it any further.'

'I see. Then will you please explain – or come with me now, to Robin –'

'I'm not coming,' said Aubrey savagely. 'I don't want any more scenes. You've won – Robin's won. She isn't my wife.'

'Ah!' said Christopher under his breath.

'She fainted in the taxi coming with me from Victoria,' continued Aubrey sullenly. 'I had her taken into the hotel as my wife, and nursed back to health. But I didn't touch a hair of her prudish little head. She's just as innocent as the day she left Little Priory.'

Christopher drew a deep breath.

'Go on,' he said. 'And what about Paris? The truth, mind you, and nothing but the truth.'

'She went with me to Paris,' said Aubrey, shrugging his shoulders. 'But she didn't live with me; she ran away from me. I don't believe she ever really cared for me. At any rate, she's all you believe her to be, and you're welcome to her. Now do you want any more?'

Christopher released his arm.

'No. I want no more. I can only say that if any man deserves to be thrashed publicly, you do.'

Aubrey gave a short, angry laugh.

'Oh, don't be dramatic, Quest. I've done what used to be called the "right thing" now, haven't I?' He laughed again. He was furiously angry because he was defeated. 'Anyhow I'm going to clear out. I've had enough of women. Marry your dear Robin and be happy.'

If Christopher had felt stronger and better he would have kicked Aubrey Mauldron there and then. But as it was he felt giddy and weak and at the back of his mind danced the glorious, relieving thought that Robin was innocent and wronged – that there was nothing now between them – no shadow of doubt – no ugly suspicion.

He stumbled down the steps and hailed a passing taxi.

'The Coherne Hotel, Bayswater,' he said.

CHAPTER XII

WHEN Christopher Quest marched into the cheap Bayswater Hotel where Robin had fled for refuge, and inquired for her, he was told she was in her room.

'The young lady arrived rather weak and tired – has been very ill,' the manageress informed Christopher. 'I believe she's resting. Shall I tell her you're here?'

'No – I'll go up to her,' said Christopher recklessly. 'I'm her husband.'

He delighted in the lie. He was radiantly happy at the thought that he had found her – that he could tell her everything was all right.

The manageress gave a shocked exclamation.

'Her husband? But she's called Miss Frayne!'

Christopher threw the woman one of his irresistible, boyish smiles.

'To tell you the truth, she's run away from me,' he said. 'But I'm going to take her home again right now.'

'Dear me,' said the manageress, thrilled. 'Fancy that, now.'

Two minutes later, Christopher was knocking on the door of No. 25. Robin's voice said: 'Come in.' And he walked straight in.

Robin felt wretchedly weak and sick after her escape from Aubrey, but she had made up her mind that she must look for a job at once. When Christopher entered she was examining the 'Situations Vacant' column of several daily papers. Christopher thought he had never seen a more pathetic sight. Such a white, weary figure, with a ruffled, dark head, and big, sad eyes. Papers strewn all over the bed.

She stared at Christopher as though at a ghost. The shock of seeing him made her almost speechless. Then she said:

'Chris – *Chris!*'

'Robin!' he said. 'Oh, my poor little Robin!'

And the next moment his arm was round her, holding her close, close to his heart. His warm, swift kisses fell on her cheeks, her hair, her eyes.

'Robin – my dear – my sweet!'

She put her arms about his neck and pulled the fair head down to hers.

'Chris – it can't be true – it can't – '

'What can't?'

'That you're here.'

'But I am, my sweet. And I'm never going to leave you again.'

'But how did you get here? How did you know?'

Christopher told her. He smoothed the hair back from her hot forehead and told her what Aubrey Mauldron had said.

'The man's a hound of the worst type, but my dear – if only I'd known in the beginning – if only you'd told me, down at Little Priory – '

'I didn't think it any use,' said Robin. 'Darling Chris – I thought you might say you believed what I had to tell you – but there'd always have been the doubt between us.'

'I don't think so, Robin. I know you. And even if you had stayed the night with that swine' – he set his teeth – 'it'd have been his fault. You were only a kid.'

She gave a weak laugh and put one of his hands against a cheek that was wet with tears.

'Darling – it was only three months ago.'

'You're still a kid. A poor little baby. The only thing I want you to tell me is that you love me a thousand times more than you did Mauldron.'

She looked at him with bright, intense eyes.

'Chris – ten thousand times more – ten million times more. Oh, my dearest, my dearest – you must believe that.'

'I do,' he said. 'And now you've got to get fit and marry me by special licence, and we'll get away from everyone we've ever known, and forget the world.'

'But your people – '

126

'My people, including Doria Southway, treated you damn badly while I was ill. It's their fault if I don't consider their feelings now.'

'Make allowances for your mother, Chris. She loves you very much.'

'It's like you to take her part – you blessed saint.'

'Oh, Chris –' She shut her eyes and drew one of his hands up to her lips. 'I'm not a saint, and I never will be. I'm very human.'

'Adorably human. Sweet – we're a couple of wrecks at the moment, and it's pretty evident to me that we want a rest, a change, and a happy holiday, and that's what we're going to have – right away.'

'It's too good to be true,' she whispered. Then suddenly the dimples that he found so attractive appeared in the pale young face. 'Chris – how on earth did you get up here – into my room like this?'

'I'm behaving as badly as Mauldron, darling. I told the spinster in charge of this hotel that you'd run away from me and I – your husband – had come to take you home.'

'Oh, *Chris!*'

'Well, what about it sweetheart?'

'Home's where you are, Chris.'

'Right. Then I'll get that licence tomorrow, and the day after, will you join me at *my* hotel and help me find a home for both of us?'

'Yes,' said Robin, shutting her eyes rapturously. '*Yes!*'

And there was nothing much more to be said after that. Only long kisses and that long silence which is so full, so satisfying to lovers, and a sudden vision unfolding before Robina Frayne. A vision of Chris, and a cottage, and a garden full of flowers; a summer night of moonshine and starlight, and a dream-come-true.

Other novels by Denise Robins
in Coronet Books

All these books are available at your bookshop or newsagent, or can be ordered direct from the publisher. Just tick the titles you want and fill in the form below.

....

CORONET BOOKS, Cash Sales Department, Kernick Industrial Estate, Penryn, Cornwall.

Please send cheque or postal order. No currency, and allow 5p per book (4p per book on orders of five copies and over) to cover the cost of postage and packing in U.K., 6p per copy overseas.

Name ....

Address ....

....

....